William D'Acry Haley

Philp's Washington Described

A complete view of the American Capital and the District of Columbia

William D'Acry Haley

Philp's Washington Described
A complete view of the American Capital and the District of Columbia

ISBN/EAN: 9783337230869

Printed in Europe, USA, Canada, Australia, Japan

Cover: Foto ©Andreas Hilbeck / pixelio.de

More available books at **www.hansebooks.com**

PHILP'S
WASHINGTON DESCRIBED.

A COMPLETE VIEW OF

THE AMERICAN CAPITAL,

AND THE

DISTRICT OF COLUMBIA;

WITH MANY NOTICES,

HISTORICAL, TOPOGRAPHICAL, AND SCIENTIFIC,

OF THE

SEAT OF GOVERNMENT.

EDITED BY WILLIAM D. HALEY.

NEW YORK:
RUDD & CARLETON.
PHILADELPHIA: J. B. LIPPINCOTT & CO.   BOSTON: CROSBY, NICHOLS, LEE & CO.
WASHINGTON: PHILP & SOLOMONS.
1861.

CONTENTS.

CHAPTER IV.

LEGISLATIVE DEPARTMENTS OF THE GOVERNMENT.

CHAPTER V.

JUDICIAL DEPARTMENT OF THE GOVERNMENT.

CHAPTER VI.

GOVERNMENTAL AND NATIONAL ESTABLISHMENTS.

CHAPTER VII.

ETIQUETTE.

CHAPTER VIII.

CITY OF WASHINGTON.

CHAPTER IX.

GEORGETOWN.

CHAPTER X.

PLACES OF INTEREST NEAR THE SEAT OF GOVERNMENT.

1*

LIST OF ILLUSTRATIONS.

EDITOR'S PREFACE.

THERE are two exigencies in authorship equally perplexing: one is, the absence of a theme when composition is necessary; the other, the presence of a theme which must be condensed within certain limits. Comparatively exhaustive as, it is hoped, the following pages will be found, the things of which they treat require much more extensive elaboration. Nowhere, probably, can there be found so small a territory embracing as many objects of interest as are contained in the District of Columbia; and yet the citizens of the United States have but a faint conception of the value of the seat of government, and foreign nations still cling to the belief that the distances between the public buildings exceed their magnificence.

The critics must decide the literary merits of this work; but we respectfully submit that, in accuracy of statement, it is to be relied upon; because none but acknowledged literary and scientific authorities have been consulted, and those have been carefully compared.

Great pains have been bestowed upon the classification of topics; and it is believed that the volume will be equally acceptable to the residents in the District, and to those who feel that the history of a nation's political Capital is the best register of national progress.

The editor trusts that his work may vindicate its right to existence, and prove a sufficient record of the love and pains of its parentage; and he acknowledges his indebtedness to many gentlemen for assistance, especially to C. W. HINMAN, Esq., Baron de OSTEN SACKEN, Professors HENRY, BAIRD, FORD, GILL, ULKE, and JILLSON, and Doctors GALE, FORCE, and FOREMAN. It is due to T. U. WALTER, Esq., to mention that the engraving of the capital of a column, on page 122, was designed by that gentleman.

PHILP'S

WASHINGTON DESCRIBED.

CHAPTER I.

GEOGRAPHY AND NATURAL HISTORY.

THE District of Columbia, as originally ceded to the Federal Government, by the States of Virginia and Maryland, contained ten miles square, or one hundred square miles; but when, in 1846, Alexandria was retroceded to Virginia, the area of the District was reduced to about sixty square miles. The Capitol lies in 38° 52' 20" north latitude, and 77° 0' 15" west longitude from Greenwich. The Observatory, from which the American meridian is computed, lies in 38° 53' 39".25 north latitude, and 77° 2' 48" (5 hours, 8 minutes, 11.2 seconds) west longitude.

The District of Columbia is bounded by the State of Maryland on the east, north, and west, and by the Potomac river and Virginia on the south. The distances from the seat of government, of some of the principal cities in the Union, are as follows:—

	Miles		Miles
Albany	376	Milwaukie	700
Baltimore	39	Mobile	1,000
Boston	432	New Orleans	1,200
Charleston	544	New York	226
Chicago	763	Philadelphia	136
Cincinnati	497	Richmond	120
Detroit	526	St. Louis	850

2

CAPTAIN JOHN SMITH'S DESCRIPTION OF CHESAPEAKE BAY.

"There is but one entrance by sea into this country, and that is at the mouth of a very goodly bay, eighteen or twenty miles broad. The cape on the south is called Cape Henry, in honor of our most noble Prince. * * * The north cape is called Cape Charles, in honor of the worthy Duke of York. The island before it, Smith's Island, by the name of the discoverer. * * * This bay lyeth north and south, in which the water floweth near 200 miles, and has a channel for 140 miles; of depth, between six and fifteen fathoms, holding a breadth, for the most part, ten or fourteen miles. From the head of the bay to the northwest, the land is mountainous, and so in a manner from thence by a southwest line, so that the more southward, the farther off from the bay are those mountains; from which fall certain brooks, which, after, come to fine navigable rivers. These run from the northwest into the southeast, and so into the west side of the bay, where the fall of every river is within twenty or fifteen miles one of the other. The mountains are of divers nature, for, at the head of the bay, the rocks are of a composition like mill-stones; some of marble, &c., and many pieces like bristol, we found as thrown down by the water from those mountains; for in Winter they are covered with much snow, and, when it dissolves, the water falls with such violence that it causes great inundation in some narrow valleys, which is scarce perceived, being once in the river. These waters wash from the rocks such glistening tinctures, that the ground in some places seemeth as gilded, where both the rocks and the earth are so splendid to behold that better inducement than ours might have been persuaded they contain more than probabilities. The vesture of the earth in most places doth manifestly prove the nature of the soil to be lusty and very rich. * * * In Summer, no place affordeth more plenty of sturgeon ; nor, in Winter, more abundance of fowl in the time of frost. I took once fifty-two sturgeon at a draught, at another sixty-eight. From the latter part of May till the end of June are taken few, and they are but a yard long. From then, till the middle of September, they are seldom less than two yards long ; and in four or five hours, with one net, there were ordinarily taken seven or eight. In the small rivers there are, all the year, plenty of small fish ; so that, with hooks, those that would take pains have sufficient. * * * Such great and well proportioned men are seldom seen, for they seem like giants to the English, yea, and to their neighbors, yet seemed of an honest and simple disposition, and, with much ado, restrained from adoring us as God."

GEOLOGY.

Washington and Georgetown, and, indeed, the whole District, is underlaid with gneiss rock, the trend of which is nearly east and west. Throughout the City of Washington and its suburbs the rock is covered to a greater or less depth with a tertiary formation of mineral matter, a considerable part of which is drift. The drift in some places consists of sandstone, limestone, jasper rock, quartz in boulders, pebbles, gravel, sand, clay, and loam. The mixture of loam and clay often abounds in a peculiar state of aggregation, as if the clay and loam had been at first separate, and in masses of considerable size, and

these ultimately thrown into a confused mass. Such is the character of the ground on English Hill, on East Branch, just below the Navy Yard, about the brick kilns, between the Navy Yard and the arsenal. This character of the tertiary is well adapted to the manufacture of brick, and constitutes the basis of this manufacture in Washington. The parts A, A, A, in the sketch, represent the gneiss rock, which was originally compact and, apparently, durable, and, as found in the neighborhood of Little Falls, some two miles above Georgetown, it is extensively quarried, and used in cellar and foundation walls, and other coarse work. It splits in two directions nearly at right angles to each other, which fits it for faced work with little labor. There is one peculiarity in this rock, however, which renders it very uncertain as a durable stone. In certain locations it goes to decay rapidly, and disintegrates entirely in a few years. The rock, as it exists on the Virginia shore of the Potomac at Little Falls, has so broken down along the road side that a rod may be forced into it in some places for two feet from the surface, by the thrust of the arm. It is not so throughout, but only in certain localities. The cause of this peculiarity has not been investigated. It is proper to say, with regard to the underlying gneiss rock of the Potomac valley, that the rock does not appear at the surface at all the places marked A ; but, from the appearance and features of the surface, it is evidently there ; and it contributes to make and shape the contour of the surface. To the eastward and north-eastward, the valley of the East Branch constitutes a flat river bottom which receives the drain from the contiguous banks and lands. As we proceed along the east side of the Potomac, from the Capitol toward the north and northwest, the rock first makes its appearance parallel with the river (that is, the trend or line of the ridge of the rocks), in the vicinity of Pennsylvania Avenue where it crosses Rock Creek, which forms the dividing line between Washington and Georgetown.

Georgetown lies virtually at the head of tide-water, although the salt water does not ascend nearer than forty or fifty miles. Georgetown, therefore, is at the junction of the tertiary and primary rocks, and at the last fall of the river, before it plunges into positive tide-water. Georgetown may be said to rest on the primary gneiss, while Washington, though evidently resting on the same base, has its substratum so low, by the dip of the rock beneath the surface, that it may be properly, and is generally, called tertiary, on account of the accumulation of clays, sands, and drift that have been piled upon it to the depth of many hundred feet, and which belong to the deposits of the tertiary formation. No considerable borings in the way of artesian wells have been made, so as to

decide at what depths the rock is reached from the surface in the different parts of the City of Washington.
Suffice it to say, that the results obtained from such excavations as have been made by digging wells and cutting
down hills show a great variety of mineral matter and
of successions of deposit.

We will speak first of the deposits as geological, then
of the mineral matter, referring to the sources of it.   At
the lowest point penetrated, say 40 to 50 feet, we find
successive beds of clays, sands, peaty earth, exogenous
woods, in fragments, and silicified; others not silicified, but
in a lignitous state; others containing pyrites of iron; but
these are confined to certain localities covered with water.
In drier parts, where pyrites have been formed, the pyrites have undergone a decomposition, and the iron has
become peroxydized, and shapen in various forms, according to that of the original nucleus.   Thus we frequently
obtain, in excavating, balls of iron, sand, or clay, like can-
non-balls in form, but very light; and on breaking them
open we find within the remains of a pine-knot or other
vegetable matter, around which the sulphate of alumina or
of iron had originally formed, on the carbonaceous matter.
Subsequently the sulphur of the compound has been removed, and left the iron predominating in the state of
iron-sand cemented together.

In 1856, or thereabout, in excavating I Street, at the
junction of New Jersey Avenue, a log of silicified wood
was removed at a depth of about 22 feet below the original surface.   It was fully silicified throughout, with the
strong marks of the grain of exogenous wood, of structure
closely resembling the oak.   It had crystals of quartz on
its surface in great abundance.

The various strata of these deposits, especially the lowest, had evidently been deposited in quiet waters, as at the bottoms of lagoons or ponds, or stagnant pools where were first sand or gravel, then clays, then peat matters charged with iron ; then, perhaps, some of these deposits repeated, and finally covered with ten or fifteen feet of drift. In all cases, the drift is on the top, and is very irregular in its character, generally consisting of masses or clumps of broken-up clay and loam, and pebbles, irregularly thrown together; and these constitute the mass of earth as found in the excavations of the streets in Washington and its suburbs. Clay, however, is the predominating earth throughout almost the whole District where the rock is covered with tertiary matters. The iron, being quite abundant and soluble in the carbonic acid of the air, is absorbed in the falling rain and surface water into the ground, and gives an iron deposit in nearly all water drawn from pumps and wells, conferring a degree of hardness which renders it objectionable for domestic uses. The debris of the broken-down gneiss rock gives a clear, micaceous loam, that does not abound in clay ; hence, the hills about the District are more like other primary lands. The distinctive character of the mineral matter found in the tertiary of the District has been the result, not of one uniform action, but of several successive and different actions, and with long intervals between, in which peat and other vegetable growth has accumulated these followed by sudden inundation of sands or gravels, &c., and these at last by vast accumulations of drift. In all cases, the deposit was from an older formation ; and we find amongst the drift limestone and sandstone, in pebbles of various sizes, in rolled masses. In the latter, the *Delthyris arenosa*, the peculiar fossil of the Oriskany sandstone, in the New York system, has been repeatedly identified. But from-what locality this fossil has come, is unknown. A sandstone has been also found amongst this drift, perfectly resembling, in granular structure, mineral matter, and shade of color, the Seneca sandstone, of which the Smithsonian building is constructed. These resemblances, although sufficient to indicate probability of source, are not sufficient to identify it. The mineral contents, beside those already named, are mostly siliceous, and such as would result from the debris of the gneiss of the substratum of the neighborhood

HYDROGRAPHY.

The principal water-course in the District of Columbia is the Potomac River, which, taking its rise in the Alleghany Mountains, receives the waters of several important streams, and, after a winding course of about four hundred miles, discharges into Chesapeake Bay. The principal tributaries of the Potomac are the Shenandoah, the Monocacy, the Conococheague, and the Anacostia, or eastern branch of the Potomac.

The tide-water of the Potomac ceases at the Little Falls, a romantic succession of cascades, three miles above Georgetown. At the Washington Navy Yard the average tide rises three feet, the Spring tide three and a half feet, and the neap two and a half feet. The southerly winds have a marked effect upon the height and continuance of the tides, and periodical freshets swell the volume of water. The Potomac is navigable as far as Greenleaf's Point, for the largest class of vessels, as is evidenced by the approach of the British squadron when the Capital was captured, and by the fact that the American frigate Minnesota, which was built at the Washington Navy Yard, was safely launched and successfully navigated down the river to Chesapeake Bay. Between the Navy Yard and Georgetown the channel has been filled up with denudations from the upper valley of the Potomac, but it has been recently dredged by the corporations of Washington and Georgetown, at a heavy cost, and is now navigated by the large steamers which ply between Washington and New York.

Within the District, the principal tributaries of the Potomac are Rock Creek, which separates Washington, on the west, from Georgetown, and the Anacostia, or east branch of the Potomac. The latter is a tidal stream, once capable of bearing large ships, and, until within a few years, navigated by a smaller class of vessels as far as Bladensburgh.

The scientific surveys of the Potomac have not yet been sufficiently accurate to determine the velocity of the current created by the tidal wave, and other important data require the researches of the United States Coast Survey. From the Potomac the following marketable fishes are obtained, amongst which the shad and herring, because of their abundance, are, in an economical point of view, the most important: cat-fish, chub, eel, gar, herring, perch (white and yellow), pike, rock-fish, shad, sturgeon, suckers, sun-fish, and various other small species. Of sturgeon, specimens have been caught weighing over three hundred pounds.

2*

ZOOLOGY.

Mammalia.—Whatever may have been the number of species of mammals inhabiting the District of Columbia in former times, the greater portion of them yet maintain a more or less permanent footing. Of those which formerly roamed over its surface, the wild cat (*Lynx rufus*), the panther, the American wolf, the black bear, the beaver, and perhaps the elk (*Cervus Canadensis*), are the only ones not found here at the present time, and it is even quite probable that the first-mentioned species still exists as a straggler. It is not probable that the buffalo ever lived in this region; the deer is not rare in the old ten-mile square; the otter even now is occasionally met with along the Potomac River, while foxes, rabbits, field mice, muskrats, and other species are more abundant than ever.

As far as accurate data are at our command, the following appear to be the characteristic features of the mammalian fauna of the District:

Of the *Cheiroptera*, or bats, about six species have hitherto been found. Of the *Insectivora*, there are three species of shrew mice, one of them a rare and little-known one, *Sorex personatus.* The common mole, *Scalops aquaticus*, and the star-nosed mole, *Condylura cristata*, also occur,—the latter here finding its southern limit.

Of the *Carnivora*, two species of fox, the red and the gray, are abundant. The ermine weasel, *Putorius Noveboracensis*, although not rare, is not often taken. It is too far south here to assume its white, winter dress,—remaining brown the whole year. The mink (*Putorius vison*) was also common until the rise in the value of its fur caused increased attention to its pursuit and capture. The otter has been already referred to as occasionally found in the Potomac. The skunk (*Mephitis mephitica*) is almost as much a nuisance as ever. The raccoon is frequently brought into market, as is also the opossum (*Didelphys Virginiana*), the single representative of the *Marsupialia*.

Of the *Rodentia*, or gnawing animals, there are five kinds of squirrels, including the striped or ground squirrel and the flying squirrel. The most interesting species is the cat squirrel (*Sciurus cinereus*), a very large, heavy kind, occurring in different varieties of color, as red, gray, and black. It is confined to a limited area in Virginia, Maryland, Pennsylvania, Delaware, and New Jersey. The woodchuck (*Arctomys monax*) belongs to the same family with the squirrel.

Of other families of rodents, the jumping mouse, *Jaculus Hudsonius*, finds here nearly its southern limit. There are two long-tailed wild mice, *Hesperomys leucopus* and *Nuttalli;* and it is probable that the wood rat, *Neotoma Floridana*, was once found here.* Of the short-tailed field mice, one (*Arvicola riparia*) is the most abundant, the *A. pinetorum*, or pine mouse, being rare. The muskrat, the common rabbit (*Lepus sylvaticus*), and the Virginia deer, the latter the only ruminant, complete the catalogue.

Three species of rats and one of mice have been introduced into the district from Europe, making the total number of species now found to be 37. Adding at least five species formerly abundant, but now exterminated, we have 42 in all.

* It has very recently been sent to the Smithsonian Institution, from Loudon County, Virginia.

Ornithology.—The District of Columbia, by reason of its situation between the northern and southern portions of the country, seems designed by nature to be the locality where the species peculiar to each section may meet, as, for a similar reason, it has been selected to be the political centre of the United States. Its situation with regard to east and west may be said to be, in a measure, central— equally distant on the one hand from the ocean with which it is connected by the broad waters of Chesapeake Bay and the Potomac River, and on the other from the extensive ranges of mountains lying directly to the westward. If, in addition to the advantages resulting from this central location, we take into consideration those arising from the varied character of its surface, and that of the adjacent country, we cannot but be struck with its peculiar adaptation to the habits of many and various species. We may expect to find within its limits a large proportion of the birds composing the eastern fauna of our country. And this, indeed, is the case. With the exception of those hardy birds fitted by nature to endure the rigorous climate of the high latitudes, which seldom or never leave the hyperborean regions of the north, and those delicate species which are Summer visitants to our southern States from more tropical countries, there are few birds composing the eastern fauna which are not, at certain seasons, to be found within its borders. It forms the natural limit to the further progress of many more southern birds.

The Summer red-bird (*Pyranga æstiva*), the cardinal grosbeak (*Cardinalis Virginianus*) the celebrated Mocking-bird (*Mimus polyglottus*), Henslow's Bunting (*Coturniculus Henslowi*), and some others, do not proceed much beyond it; while it restricts the further southern migration of such birds as the white crowned sparrow (*Zonotrichia leucophrys*), the red cross bill (*Curvirostra Americana*), the pine finch (*Chrysomitris pinus*), the lesser red poll linnet (*Aegiothus linaria*), &c. Although so limited in area, the District of Columbia possesses, in woods, meadows, marshes, and streams, a character of surface so varied that every class of birds can find the peculiar situations they were designed to frequent. Its proximity to Chesapeake Bay, that great Winter resort for nearly all the ducks and other sea-fowl which retire to the far north to breed, and its situation along the Potomac River, one of its greatest tributaries, causes all the species to be found within its limits. But the incessant persecutions to which these birds are subjected have so materially decreased their numbers that they are every year becoming scarcer; and the great body of those that are left, intimidated by incessant harassing, have removed to the numerous bays and inlets along the sinuosities of the Carolinian and other southern shores. Its position along the banks of the Potomac affords the sandy and muddy flats which the sand-pipers and the other smaller waders frequent; while the extensive marshes and swampy tracts, where the wild oats (*Zizania aquatica*) grow in profusion, furnish suitable food to the thousands of rail, blackbirds, and reed-birds, which at certain seasons frequent those localities in immense numbers. Along the beautiful little stream known as "Rock Creek" are many shady, secluded hills, which, in the Spring and Autumn, abound with warblers, thrushes, and the smaller fly-catchers; while over its waters are to be heard at all times, during the Summer, the loud rattling of the kingfisher, the "peet-weet" of the spotted landpiper, and the green heron is seen to fly slowly along beneath the overhanging branches. The thick cedars which border this creek are favorite resorts of the beautiful cardinal grosbeak or Virginia red-bird (*Cardinalis Virginianus*), so well known and justly celebrated both for the beauty of his plumage, and the richness and melody of his pleasing song. There are also extensive meadows to be found in every direction, which furnish a suitable abode for the lark (*Sturnella magna*), the black-throated bunting (*Euspiza Americana*), and the various species of sparrows which are never found but in such situations. Though the number of birds resident throughout the year, and which breed here, is considerable, they are few in comparison with the numbers that pass through the District during their Spring and Autumn migrations, and those which are merely visitors during the Summer and Winter months—the former from a more southern climate, the latter from the northern regions. As an example of the number of birds which pass through on their way to the north to breed, we may cite the wood warblers, or *Dendroicas*. Of the twelve species which are found more or less abundantly in Spring and Autumn, but *three*, the common Summer yellow bird (*D. æstiva*), the pine-creeping (*D. pinus*), and the prairie warbler (*D. discolor*), breed here at all, and the last of these is rare. Again, of the six species of thrushes (Genus *Turdus*) which are abundant during their migrations, but *two*, the robin (*T. migratorius*), and the wood thrush (*T. mustelinus*), remain during the Summer. The same might be said with reference to the smaller fly-catchers, the sandpipers, &c. Those birds which visit us in the Summer are for the most part the young of species which breed further south, and are generally observed in the months of July and August. Such is the case with regard to the small blue heron (*Florida coerulea*), the white ibis (*Ibis alba*), the great white egret (*Herodias egretta*), and some others. Among our rarer Winter visitants are the white crowned sparrow (*Zonotrichia leucophrys*), the great northern shrike or butcher-bird (*Collyrio borealis*), and in severe Winters the snowy owl (*Nyctea nivea*), and probably the snow bunting (*Plectrophanes nivalis*). The occurrence of a few other species in this vicinity must be looked upon as purely accidental and dependent on no fixed habit of the bird. Thus, during a violent easterly storm a few years ago, the Potomac was covered with multitudes of Mother Cary's chickens (*Thalassidroma Leachii*), which had been forced out of their usual course by the gale. The single instance of the occurrence of the ground dove (*Chamaepelia passerina*) in this vicinity must be regarded as equally accidental. Two hundred and thirty-six species of birds have been collected in the District.

Herpetology.—Considering the small extent of the District of Columbia, there are several features of much interest in regard to its reptiles. The number of species is quite large, amounting, as will be seen, to over fifty, some of them being very rare. As in other departments of zoology, there is a mixture of the northern and southern faunas, although the prevailing character of the herpetology is, perhaps, southern rather than northern.

Of the turtles, some of the species extend their range over wide areas of the country, while others are much more restricted. The well-known diamond-backed or salt-water terrapin (*Emys terrapin*) is common in the lower brackish waters of the Potomac River, and probably comes but rarely of its own accord into the District. As a delicacy this species takes rank with the canvas-back duck. Another terrapin, the *Emys rubriventris*, or red-bellied terrapin, very common in the Washington market, attains a large size, and is much esteemed as an article of food. The snapping turtle (*Chelonura serpentina*) is also frequently found on the stalls of the dealers. The total number of species of turtles found within the District is about nine. One of them, the *Emys picta*, finds here nearly its southern limit, while the *E. terrapin* and *rubriventris*, both tide-water species, are not met with much further to the eastward.

Of the true lizards, with scales, three species only have yet been found in the District, though one or two more may yet be detected. One of them, the *Sceloporus undulatus*, a rough, brown species, with blue neck, may frequently be seen running along the fences by the road-side. The six-lined lizard (*Cnemidophorus sexlineatus*) seldom occurs further north. The blue-tailed lizard, with five white lines (*Plestiodon*), is often found in wood-piles.

The list of serpents found about Washington is quite extensive, embracing at least twenty-one species. The most important of these is the deadly copperhead snake (*Ancistrodon contortrix*), not uncommon about the Little Falls. The rattlesnake is not now known to inhabit the District, though doubtless once a resident. Other serpents are the well-known black snake, various striped or garter snakes, water snakes, etc. Blowing vipers or hog-nosed snakes, erroneously believed to be venomous, are some-times met with. The slender green snake (*Leptophis æstivus*), characteristic of a southern fauna, as also *Lam-*

propeltis getula, the chain-snake, are quite abundant.   The rare *L. clerica* has several times been met with.

Of the group of frogs and toads nine species are known, of all sizes, from the huge bull-frog, to the cricket-frog not larger than a blue-bottle fly, and very abundant in the slashes north of the city, where its singular note, resembling the sound of two pebbles struck rapidly together, may constantly be heard in the Summer season.   The most curious species of all, however, is the spade-footed toad (*Scaphiopus Holbrookii*), which though quite abundant is very rarely seen, owing to its remaining buried up in sand or loose earth almost all the time, and coming out only during wet and stormy nights.   The spade-shaped attachment to the hind feet is used to scoop out the earth, into which it speedily sinks and is covered up.

Of the remaining group of reptiles—the salamanders, or water lizards, with smooth, naked, slimy skins, and living under damp logs, or stones, or in the water—there are about ten species, making fifty-two species, in all, of reptiles actually collected in the District.

It may be well to mention here, by way of correcting a popular impression in the vicinity of Washington, that, with the exception of the copperhead (unless the rattlesnake still exists), there are no poisonous reptiles whatever in the District.   However threatening in their actions the blowing vipers or adders, the black snakes, the green snakes, or the water snakes may be, all, with the exceptions mentioned, are entirely destitute of venomous properties, although the scratch from their teeth might produce a festering sore, similar to that sometimes caused by a pin or needle.   The lizards of all kinds, whether of the kind popularly known as scorpions by the country people, or others, are absolutely and positively harmless, few, if any, being able even to scratch by their bite enough to tear the skin.

Ichthyology.—The fishes of the District present but few peculiarities; almost all of the species belong to genera that are represented in the northern as well as the southern States, species characteristic of the two sections of the country being here intermingled. Representatives of three and perhaps four of the sub-classes into which fishes may be divided are found.

Of the true fishes, or Teleostei, there are numerous species which represent many genera. Some salt-water, estuary, and migratory species ascend as far up as the Falls of the Potomac. The "rock-fish," or "striped bass" (*Roccus lineatus*, Gill), and the "white perch" (*Morone Americana*, Gill), are the best known and the most common. Both of them, but more especially the rock-fish, are much angled for. The white perch is caught principally in the Spring months, and the rock-fish in the Summer.

The "sunfishes" (*Lepomis* or *Pomotis*) are also quite numerous in the streams of the District.

Of the Etheostomoids, a family peculiar to North America, representatives have been described, by Dr. Girard, of several generic groups. These are *Arlina effulgens, Estrella atro-maculata* of Girard, the *Percina nebulosa* of Haldeman, and perhaps the *Hadropterus maculatus* of Girard. All of them are small fishes with two dorsal fins, the first of which is supported by slender spines. They appear to represent in the fresh waters of the United States the Gobioids of the Old World, and to be nearly allied to them.

The "bill-fish" (*Belone truncata* of Lesueur), which belongs to the family of Scomberesocoids, is occasionally caught below the Falls. It is readily distinguished by its snipe-like bill, the dorsal and anal fins placed opposite each other and far back, and by the small scales.

The family of Cyprinodonts is represented by several species confounded under the names of "minnows" and "killie-fish." They are distinguished by their depressed head covered with large scales, and the posterior position of their small dorsal fin. All of them are of small size.

The family of the true Cyprinoids, as now restricted, has many species, belonging to a number of different genera. The *Rhinichthys* is a small fish, with a prominent snout, and a blackish band along the side. Two species, belonging respectively to the genera *Cyprinella* and *Clinostomus* of Dr. Girard, are among the most interesting, as they are the most eastern representatives of those genera known. They are favorite ornaments of fresh-water aquaria. The common "shiner" belongs to this family, and is the *Luxilus chrysoleucas* of naturalists.

The "suckers" belong to a family very nearly allied to the preceding. Two species are quite abundant in the streams of the District. One is a *Catastomus*, and has a lateral line, or perforated row of scales along the sides, and the other, destitute of such a line, belongs to the genus *Moxostoma*.

The above-named species belong to one order to which the name of Teleocephali has been given; the Cyprinoids and Catastomoids form a sub-order called *Eventognathi ;* the Cyprinodonts belong to the Physostomi; and the remainder to the sub-order of Physoclysti.

Of the "cat-fishes" (*Nematognathi*), there are several species belonging to the genera *Amiurus* or *Pimelodus* of many naturalists, and *Noturus*. The latter is called "stone cat." The wound inflicted by its spines becomes excessively painful, and has even been known to produce death.

Of the sub-class of Ganoids, the "garpike" (*Lepidosteus*) and "sturgeon" (*Accipenser*) are abundant near Washington. They belong to two different orders. The former is easily distinguished by its rhombic enameled scales.

A species of shark occasionally ascends the Potomac River. We then have a representative of the sub-class of Elasmobranchii, and of the order of Plagiostomes.

The lamprey (*Petromyzon*), belonging to the sub-class of Dermopteri and order of Marsipobranchii, is said to be also an inhabitant of the District.

Entomology.—The District has its entomological fauna in common with Maryland and northern Virginia, both of which belong to what is commonly called by entomologists the region of the Middle States. Those species only of this region which are peculiar to mountains or to the seashore are naturally wanting in the District. It may be said in general that the soil of the District is not favorable to insect life, as it consists chiefly of clay, sand, and boulders, and becomes too hard and dry in Summer. During the hot season, the insects do not find moisture enough to sustain their existence, and the hardness of the soil prevents them from seeking shelter under ground. The consequence is, that although the number of *species* occurring here is considerable, the number of *specimens* is not in proportion. A few more favored localities form an exception to this rule; a walk along Rock Creek and Piney Branch, towards the slashes, where the latter takes its origin, may reward the collector for his exertions. The same may be said of some localities beyond the Eastern Branch, in the valleys between the hills on that side of the river.

Conchology, etc.—The conchology of the District is interesting, the number (86) of shells in its fauna being large for so small a tract of country, which is in consequence of the great variety of stations. Fresh-water shells are particularly numerous, since we have not only a large river with all kinds of shore, muddy below, and rocky above Georgetown; but many smaller streams of all sizes, affording stations for a great variety of species. There are 50 species of fresh-water shells, 18 bivalves (of the genera *Cyclas*, *Pisidium*, *Unio*, *Alasmodon*, and *Anodon*), and 32 univalves (*Ancylus*, *Lymnea*, *Physa*, *Planorbis*, *Melania*, *Anculosa*, *Paludina*, *Amnicola*, and *Valvata*). The Unios are best obtained in the still waters of the canal, at the annual drawing-off of the water. The *Anculosae* and *Paludinae* are very pretty shells, and are best found at low-water mark on rocks at the Little Falls.

The land shells are of a northern rather than a southern type. There are 20 Helices, of which *H. chersina*, *concava*, *fraterna*, *gularis*, *hirsuta*, *alternata*, *lineata*, *suppressa*, *tridentata*, *and thyroidus* are the most common. *H. thyroidus* is sometimes found in gardens; all the rest live in the woods. There are also 4 *Succineae*, 1 *Bulimus*, 6 *Pupae*, 2 *Vertiginae*, and 1 *Carychium*. There is also a *Limax* and a *Philomycus*. The Limax comes out in the frosty weather of November, from among the grass in the Smithsonian grounds, and may be seen upon the gravel walks in great numbers on sunny mornings.

Of Crustacea, there are two species of cray-fish (*Cambarus*), *C. fossor* and *C. Pealei ;*—the former makes the curious mud chimneys seen in swampy places, the latter lives in the deep water of the river. In small streams there is an *Asellus*, and a *Gammarus*. In wells there is found a curious little subterranean shrimp, (*Niphargus ?*) the first ever found in America, of a genus which has excited much attention in *Europe*. Pill-bugs (*Armadillo*, *Porcellio, etc.*) are very abundant.

Dr. Girard discovered several fresh-water Planariæ in the District, of which the *Dugesia Foremanni* is one.

BOTANY.

The flora of any particular district is controlled to so great an extent by the character of the rocks and soils upon which the plants are found growing, that at the risk of repetition we must state that in the vicinity of Washington the rocks may be divided into two kinds, one lying above the points reached by the head of tide-water in the Potomac and its branches, the other embracing all the country lying south of that line and near the river. The rocks of the first division are mostly gneissoid and slate rocks, the latter consisting of micaceous and talcose slates. Into these have intruded great masses of green stone, forming the heights of Georgetown, and which may be seen in section on the canal, near Georgetown College. It may be mentioned, with regard to these rocks, that Prof. Hitchcock, when on a visit a few years since to the Great Falls of the Potomac, recognized there the same formation of old slate rocks which in the southern States and in many other parts of the world contain auriferous deposits.

The remaining division of the formations near Washington consists of drift alluvial or superficial deposits, and exhibits vast beds of gravel, boulders, sand, clay, &c. These may also be subdivided into two kinds, that which is uppermost containing transported masses enclosing Silurian or Devonian fossils, some fragments of petrified wood, and not being highly colored by the presence of ferruginous matters. The lower beds are deeply stained with iron, and show in places thick beds of a ferruginous conglomerate.

The flora of this District may be regarded as an intermingling of northern and southern forms, and exhibits but little worthy of remark which may not be likewise found along the coast region from New Jersey down to the latitude of the mouth of the Chesapeake. The great orders of *Ranunculaceæ, Cruciferæ, Leguminosæ, Rosaceæ, Umbelliferæ, Compositæ, Labiatæ, Orchideæ,* and *Gramineæ* very generally resemble in species what are found over a large circle of country around. As a notice of the genera and species individually would be out of place in this sketch, it is regarded as sufficient to indicate some of the special localities where the rarer kinds of plants may be found growing.

Among the richer spots which reward the researches of the botanist, the margins of Rock Creek and its tributaries, extending several miles in a northern direction, have been diligently visited. In the proper season, on the margin of these streams, will be found among the commoner plants two splendid lilies, two phloxes, *Pulmonaria Obolaria, Apios tuberosa,* spice wood, all the dwarf sunflowers,

Equisetum and ferns, whilst towering above all stands the great purple *Eupatorium*. One of the peculiarities of this locality is found in the marshy heads from which stream- lets issue and flow into the creek or its branches. These frequently cover several acres, and are generally shaded by large trees, interspersed among which are the *magno- lia*, poison sumach, *Chionanthus*, or fringe-tree, and the *Nyssa* or gum. These tracts are very boggy, and covered with *Sphagnum* (a moss), out of which, sometimes as early as the 15th of January, the skunk cabbage (*Symplocar- pus*) in vast numbers throws up its rich-colored spathe and flower, where also may be observed the curious young shoots of the *Osmunda*, or flowering fern, which are abundant. The most beautiful of our orchids are also to be seen later in the season in these dirty and inaccessible places, such as *Arethusa, Pogonia, Triphora, Platanthera*, and *Calopogon*. A search among the clumps of wild roses and alders will be repaid by a few plants of *Kalmia glauca, Drosera*, or sun-dew, and the rarer *Lycopodiums*. Among the hills bordering on these streams there is a locality which furnishes *Dodecatheon meadia, Batschia canescens*, and *Gualtheria procumbens*, which are exceed- ingly rare.

The stretch of country known as " the slashes," within the city limits, was long the profitable resort of botanists, but is now nearly obliterated. The soil consists of a stiff clay, which, for the most part, is spongy, from holding water nearly all the Fall, Winter, and Spring. In Sum- mer it is hard-baked and dry, except in spots occupied by small, stagnant pools. These conditions once furnished protection for many curious plants which flowered before the dry season commenced. Among these, now no longer

seen, and much lamented, was an *Utricularia*, and many
of the orchids.   Drainage, grubbing, and perpetual de-
pasturation has reduced the slashes to mere surfaces for
the production of malaria, and as proper cemeteries for
the dead animals of the city.   Enough, however, remains
to show that they were formerly covered with thickets of
bramble, sweet gum, maple, magnolia, winterberry, wild
roses, and white azaleas.   Around the clumps and roots
of these are still seen growing *Arethusa, Pogonia, Habena-
ria,* several *Violas,* with *Arnica, Asclepias,* and *Callitriche,*
in the more open spaces.

In the immediate vicinity, the flat districts on the Virginia side of the river, which are frequently overflowed
by the tides, furnish the usual array of aquatic species.
These are *Pontederia Calla, Orontium, Sagittaria,* &c.,
among the herbaceous plants, intermixed with a shrubby
growth of grapevines, *alnus,* willow, button bush, or
Cephalanthus, with *Typha,* or cat-tail, and *Zizania,* or wild
rice, to represent the grasses.   Not far distant from these,
on not much drier soil, may be seen the red and blue
Lobelia, Chelone, Bidens, or marsh marygold, a little pas-
sion-flower, and the favorite blue *Eupatorium* or *Conochin-
ium.*   Floating in the waters of Four-Mile Run may be
detected the graceful *Nymphea odorata,* and it is reported
that the great yellow *Nelumbium,* or water chinquapin,
may be gathered at Acquia Creek.   Black birch, the
silky cornel, sycamore, and hackberry, line the margins of
the swamps, and are overrun by climbers, such as trum-
pet-flower, ampelopsis, poison oak, *Celastrus,* and *Mikania.*
These overshadow half stagnant pools filled with *Myrio-
phyllum, Chara, Ceratophyllum,* and *Anacharis,* which
abound with infusorial and other microscopic forms.   In

3

the river flats there is little else than the *Valisneria,* the food of the canvas-back duck.

Among the forest trees may be found about fifteen species of oaks, mostly of the commoner sorts. Those which deserve notice as being scarce are the scrub or bear oak, the laurel oak, and Bartram's oak, or *Q. heterophylla;* the latter, upon the authority of two observers, being found within a few miles on a northeast line from the city. The chesnut, hickories, black walnut, and butternut, are common. The dwarf pine, *Pinus inops,* associated with Virginia cedar and sassafras, clothe the barren old fields, giving them an uninviting appearance. But few forest trees of original growth are now seen near the city. In private grounds or parks, on Boundary Street, in Washington, or on Georgetown Heights, may be observed some fine examples of oaks, which are preserved with commendable care. A few groves of the yellow pine are still standing among the hills, a few miles north of the city, whilst near the river margin may be seen some large specimens of American elm and linden.

On the rocky bluffs on the south side of the river, and above the Aqueduct, we have, in the early Spring, rich masses of color from the red flowers of the Judas tree, the white flowering *Amelanchier* and dogwood, in contrast with the dark foliage of the surrounding pines and cedars; and, at the water level of the same localities, the witch hazel, or *Hammamelis,* produces its yellow flowers in the Fall and its fruit in the Spring. Farther up the river, and near the Little Falls Bridge, a single settlement of *Rhododendron maximum* has been found half buried in the kalmia thickets overhanging the river.

Here we encounter the evidences of the only strange

flora which can be said to intrude into our District, most of the species of which can be traced up to the far western sources of the Potomac. They have been observed all over both sides of the river, as high up as the Great Falls, and many of them may be collected at or near High or Rock Island, about a mile above Little Falls Bridge. It will suffice to enumerate a few of the more common, viz.: *Opuntia Muscari, Phlox divaricata, Phacelia*, two species of *Sedum, Dracocephalum*, the blue *Baptisia, Jeffersonia, Trillium, Asarum*, a rare orchid, *Tipularia discolor, Erigenia bulbosa, Pentstemon*, &c. They are also accompanied by the papaw, *Dirca palustris*, or leatherwood, *Schollera* and *Lythrum*.

Among the ferns we find about twenty species, which are abundant and well grown. The only species that need be mentioned for their scarcity is the *Camptosurus*, or walking fern, at Cabin John Aqueduct Bridge, and *Asplenium augustifolium*, at High Island, before referred to.

CLIMATOLOGY.

The temperature of Washington (in the shade) ranges from 105 degrees above to twelve degrees below zero, of Fahrenheit's scale. The mean of January, the coldest month, is about 32°; and of July, the warmest month, about 77°. The mean temperature of the year is about 56°. Sudden changes of temperature are sometimes experienced, the thermometer falling 20 or 30 degrees in a few hours. These changes are not local, but may be traced, in different degrees, over a large extent of country, and come with a west or northwest wind. The river is generally closed in the early part of January, and, in very cold

Winters, heavy teams may cross on the ice. Snow rarely falls in sufficient quantities for sleighing, but sometimes admits of that mode of conveyance during several days. The Winter storms come from the west, and are preceded by a northeast wind. The prevailing wind in Winter is from the west or northwest, and in Summer from a southerly quarter. The amount of rain during a year averages about forty inches, the larger portion falling in the Summer months. The range of the barometer is nearly or quite two inches. Vegetation seems to proceed all Winter, and the migratory birds return about the first of April. Fair days are the rule, foul days form the exception, and the bad weather seems generally to commence at 3 o'clock in the afternoon or 4 in the morning.

HEALTH.

The average rate of deaths is about one in fifty; but owing to the fact that the corporation of Washington has no power to originate a penal statute, and as Congress has provided no penalty for failures to record births, marriages, and deaths, statistics upon these matters must necessarily be incomplete and unreliable. Owing to the wide streets and numerous open spaces, as well as to natural salubrity, the city and District are almost entirely exempt from epidemics; the diseases incident to compact and crowded cities are here scarcely known. There are very few deaths from malarious diseases, and the number of these is annually decreasing. A large proportion of the deaths amongst strangers for which the climate of Washington is sometimes held responsible is to be attributed to two causes,—the entire change of diet and mode of life, by which the constitution is weakened and every lurking disease strengthened, and too frequently the casting away of the moral integrity of home, by which the same result is obtained, and the victim of unusual dissipation is charged to the account of the climate of the seat of government. From the partial returns of the census of 1850, it appears that in a population of 51,687, there were only 846 recorded deaths, which would give the small percentage of 1.64.

From the report of the Commissioner of Health, it appears that during the twelve years commencing July, 1848, and ending July, 1860, the recorded deaths in the City of Washington have been as follows :—

July 1848 to June 1849,..............828	Deaths.
July 1849 to June 1850,................868	"
July 1850 to June 1851,..............914	"
July 1851 to June 1852,.............1,003	"
July 1852 to June 1853,........ 1,115	"
July 1853 to June 1854,............1,209	"
July 1854 to June 1855,...... 1,188	"
July 1855 to June 1856,.............1,081	"
July 1856 to June 1857,.............926	"
July 1857 to June 1858,.............1,108	"
July 1858 to June 1859,..............937	"
July 1859 to June 1860,..............820	"

The greatest number of deaths seems to occur in the months of July and August, but January, February, and March present formidable bills of mortality, probably owing to the vast influx of strangers during the session of Congress.

PROGRESS OF POPULATION.

It must be borne in mind, in connection with the accompanying table showing the progress of population from 1800 to 1860, that by an act of Congress, dated July 9th, 1846, Alexandria, town and county, was retro-ceded to Virginia, so that, in computing the progress of population in the District of Columbia up to 1840, the territory including Alexandria (embracing 9,969 inhabi-tants not since computed) was taken as a basis of calcu-lation.

POPULATION OF THE DISTRICT OF COLUMBIA.

Decade.	Total Population.	Increase per cent.	Decade.	Slave Population.	Increase per cent.
1800	14,093		1800	3,244	
1810	24,023	70.46	1810	5,395	. 66.3
1820	33,039	37.53	1820	6,377	18.2
1830	39,834	20.56			
1840	43,712	9.37			Decrease
1850	51,687	18.24	1830	6,119	4.04
1860	75,115	45.32	1840	4,694	23.28
			1850	3,687	21.45
			1860	3,185	13.61

CHAPTER II.

HISTORY OF THE SEAT OF GOVERNMENT.

DISTRICT OF COLUMBIA.

THE location of the seat of government was determined by Congress with much deliberation. The sessions of the old Congress were held at various places, to meet the exigencies of the occasion and humor the spirit of rivalry manifested by the different States. The subject of a permanent seat of government was first debated in Congress after the insult offered to that body in Philadelphia, in June, 1783, by a band of mutinous soldiers, who assailed the hall during session, demanding arrearages of pay. A resolution was passed, October 7, 1783, on motion of Elbridge Gerry, to erect buildings for Congress on the Delaware or the Potomac, provided a suitable district could be procured on either of those rivers, for a federal city. This resolution was subsequently modified, providing for the erection of buildings in both locations, and finally repealed, April 26, 1784. Congress met at Trenton in the following October, and appointed three commissioners to lay out a district, between two and three miles square, on the Delaware, for a federal town. At the meeting of Congress in New York, in January, 1785, an unsuccessful attempt was made to substitute the Potomac for the Delaware.   Two years later the Constitution was adopted, declaring (Article I., Section 8) "The Congress shall have power to exercise exclusive legislation, in all cases whatsoever, over such district (not exceeding ten miles square) as may, by cession of particular States and the acceptance of Congress, become the seat of government of the United States."   On the 23d of December, 1788, the Legislature of Maryland passed an act authorizing and requiring her members in Congress "to cede any district (not exceeding ten miles square) which the Congress may fix upon and accept for the seat of the government of the United States.   In 1789 Congress debated the selection of a location of the "ten miles square," carefully considering the importance of a site in the centre of territory, population, and wealth, easy of access to the west, with a convenient communication with the seaboard.

The northern members were in favor of a site on the Susquehanna, while the south favored the Delaware and Potomac; and the comparative advantages of New York, Philadelphia, Germantown, Havre de Grace, Wright's Ferry, Baltimore, and Conococheague, now Washington, were warmly discussed.   The South Carolinians opposed Philadelphia, because the Quakers favored emancipation. Large towns were objected to on the score of undue influence, while others ridiculed the idea of building palaces in the forest.   Instances of European capitals were cited in support of the claims of New York and Philadelphia. The House of Representatives passed a resolution September 5, 1789, "That the permanent seat of the government of the United States ought to be at some convenient place on the banks of the Susquehanna, in the State of Pennsylvania." This alarmed the southern members, and especially the Virginians, who strongly urged a location on the Potomac. Mr. Madison thought if the proceeding of that day had been foreseen by Virginia, that State might not have become a party to the Constitution. It was allowed by all to be a matter of vital importance to the Union. The bill to carry this resolution into effect passed the House by a vote of thirty-one to nineteen, and was amended by the Senate by inserting Germantown, Pennsylvania, in place of the location on the Susquehanna. The action of the Senate was agreed to by the House, with an amendment providing that the laws of Pennsylvania should continue in force in said district until Congress should otherwise direct. The Senate postponed the consideration of this amendment until the next session. Germantown was thus actually agreed upon, but the bill eventually failed on account of the postponement.

Following the example of the Maryland Legislature, in her act of cession, December 23, 1788, the Assembly of Virginia passed an act, December 3, 1789, ceding a district to Congress for the location of the seat of government, and also a resolution asking the coöperation of Maryland in inducing Congress to fix the seat of government upon the banks of the Potomac, and promising to advance a sum of money, not exceeding $120,000, towards erecting public buildings,—Maryland advancing a sum not less than two-fifths of that amount. Maryland acceded to the proposition, and agreed to advance the amount of money required. Other States made like offers of territory, in their anxiety to have the seat of government within their boundaries. Congress was not disposed to act upon the question, as the greatest ill feeling and a

3*

spirit of dissension had arisen among the members upon the funding act. An amendment, providing for the assumption of the State debts to the amount of twenty-one millions, was rejected in the House. The north was in favor of the assumption, and the south was opposed to the inclination to locate the seat of government on the Susquehanna.

At this critical juncture, Jefferson, then Secretary of State, and Hamilton, Secretary of the Treasury, met in conference, and proposed a compromise of the two vexed questions. Hamilton thought the north would consent to the location of the Capital on the Potomac, if the south would concede the amendment assuming the State debts. It was agreed that Jefferson should ask the interested parties to dinner next day, and propose the accommodation. The discussion took place accordingly, and it was decided to reconsider the vote upon the amendment, and two Potomac members, White and Lee, agreed to change their votes. Hamilton undertook to carry the other point with the northern members. Thus the assumption bill was passed, and also the following bill, locating the seat of government :—

An Act for establishing the temporary and permanent seat of the government of the United States.

Sec. 1. *Be it enacted, by the Senate and House of Representatives of the United States of America in Congress assembled,* That a district of territory, not exceeding ten miles square, to be located as hereafter directed, on the river Potomac, at some space between the mouths of the Eastern Branch and Conococheague, be, and the same is hereby, accepted for the permanent seat of the government of the United States : *Provided, nevertheless,* That the operation of the laws of the State within such district shall not be affected by this acceptance until the time fixed for the removal of the government thereto, and until Congress shall otherwise by law provide.

SEC. 2. *And be it further enacted,* That the President of the United States be authorized to appoint, and by supplying vacancies happening from refusals to act, or other causes, to keep in appointment as long as may be necessary, three Commissioners, who, or any two of whom, shall, under the direction of the President, survey, and by proper metes and bounds define and limit a district of territory, under the limitations above mentioned; and the district so defined, limited, and located, shall be deemed the district accepted by this act for the permanent seat of the government of the United States.

SEC. 3. *And be it enacted,* That the said Commissioners, or any two of them, shall have power to purchase or accept such quantity of land on the eastern side of the said river, within the said district, as the President shall deem proper for the use of the United States; and, according to such plans as the President shall approve, the said Commissioners, or any two of them, shall, prior to the first Monday in December, in the year one thousand eight hundred, provide suitable buildings for the accommodation of Congress, and of the President, and for the public offices of the government of the United States.

SEC. 4. *And be it enacted,* That, for defraying the expense of such purchases and buildings, the President of the United States be authorized and requested to accept grants of money.

SEC. 5. *And be it enacted,* That, prior to the first Monday in December next, all officers attached to the seat of government of the United States shall be removed to, and, until the said first Monday in December, in the year one thousand eight hundred, shall remain at, the city of Philadelphia, in the State of Pennsylvania, at which place the session of Congress next ensuing the present shall be held.

SEC. 6. *And be it enacted,* That on the said first Monday in December, in the year one thousand eight hundred, the seat of government of the United States shall, by virtue of this act, be transferred to the district and place aforesaid. And all offices attached to the said seat of government shall accordingly be removed thereto by their respective holders, and shall, after the said day, cease to be exercised elsewhere; and that the necessary expense of such removal shall be defrayed out of the duties on impost and tonnage, of which a sufficient sum is hereby appropriated.

Approved, July 16, 1790.

GEORGE WASHINGTON,
President of the United States.

The Legislature of Maryland, on the 19th of December, 1791, passed an act ratifying and confirming the cession of the District in the following terms :—

Be it enacted by the General Assembly of Maryland, That all that part of the said territory, called Columbia, which lies within the limits of this State, shall be, and the same is hereby acknowledged to be, forever ceded and relinquished to the Congress and Government of the United States, in full and absolute right and exclusive jurisdiction, as well of soil as of persons residing or to reside thereon, pursuant to the tenor and effect of the eighth section of the first article of the Constitution of Government of the United States : *Provided,* That nothing herein contained shall be so construed to vest in the United States any right of property in the soil, as to affect the rights of individuals therein, otherwise than the same shall or may be transferred by such individuals to the United States : *And provided, also,* That the jurisdiction of the laws of this State over the persons and property of individuals residing within the limits of the cession aforesaid shall not cease or determine until Congress shall by law provide for the government thereof, under their jurisdiction, in manner provided by the article of the Constitution before recited.

By an amendment, passed in Congress, March 3, 1791,

so much of the act as required the District to be located above the mouth of the Eastern Branch is repealed, and the President is authorized to make any part of the territory below the said limit and above the mouth of Hunting Creek a part of said District, so as to include a convenient part of the Eastern Branch, and of the lands lying on the lower side thereof, and also the town of Alexandria, provided that no public buildings be erected otherwise than on the Maryland side of the Potomac. Washington defined the boundaries of the District in the following amendatory proclamation :—

Whereas, by a proclamation, bearing date the 24th day of January, of this present year, and in pursuance of certain acts of the States of Maryland and Virginia, and of the Congress of the United States, therein mentioned, certain lines of experiment were directed to be run in the neighborhood of Georgetown, in Maryland, for the purpose of determining the location of a part of the territory of ten miles square, for the permanent seat of the government of the United States; and a certain part was directed to be located within the said lines of experiment, on both sides of the Potomac, and above the limit of the Eastern Branch, prescribed by the said act of Congress;

And Congress, by an amendatory act, passed on the 3d day of this present month of March, have given further authority to the President of the United States " to make any part of the said territory, below the said limit, and above the mouth of Hunting Creek, a part of the said District, so as to include a convenient part of the Eastern Branch and of the lands lying on the lower side thereof, and also the town of Alexandria ; "

Now, therefore, for the purpose of amending and completing the location of the whole of the said territory of ten miles square, in conformity with the said amendatory act of Congress, I do hereby declare and make known that the whole of the said territory shall be located and included within the four lines following, that is to say,—

Beginning at Jones' Point, being the upper cape of Hunting Creek, in Virginia, and at an angle in the outset of 45 degrees west of north, and running in a direct line ten miles, for the first line ; then beginning again at the same Jones' Point, and running another direct line at a right angle with the first, across the Potomac, ten miles, for the second line; then, from the terminations of the said first and second lines, running two other direct lines, of ten miles each, the one crossing the Eastern Branch aforesaid, and the other the Potomac, and meeting each other in a point.

And I do accordingly direct the Commissioners named under the authority of the said first-mentioned act of Congress to proceed forthwith to have the said four lines run, and by proper metes and bounds defined and limited, and thereof to make due report under their hands and seals; and the territory so to be located, defined, and limited, shall be the whole territory accepted by the said act of Congress as the District for the permanent seat of the government of the United States.

In testimony whereof, I have caused the seal of the United States to be affixed to these presents, and signed the same with my hand. Done at Georgetown aforesaid, the 30th day of March, in the year of our Lord, 1791, and of the Independence of the United States, the fifteenth.

GEORGE WASHINGTON.

In pursuance of the act of Congress, three Commissioners—Thomas Johnson, David Stuart, and Daniel Carroll—were appointed in January, 1791, to survey the District ; and, on the 15th of April, they superintended the laying of the corner-stone of the District defined by the proclamation, at Jones' Point, near Alexandria, with all the usual Masonic ceremonies of the day. The Commissioners informed Major L'Enfant, the engineer, in a letter dated at Georgetown, September 9, 1791, that they had agreed that the federal District shall be called the Territory of Columbia, and the federal city the City of Washington, and directed him to entitle his map accordingly.

Congress assumed jurisdiction over the District of Columbia by an act approved February 27, 1801.

CITY OF WASHINGTON.

In compliance with the act establishing the seat of government, the Commissioners proceeded to lay out a city. The boundaries are thus defined in the act of cession by the Legislature of Maryland, Dec. 19, 1791 :—

The President of the United States directed a city to be laid out, comprehending all the lands beginning on the east side of Rock Creek, at a stone standing in the middle of the road leading from Georgetown to Bladensburgh ; thence along the middle of said road to a stone standing on the east side of the reedy branch of Goose Creek ; thence southeasterly, making an angle of sixty-one degrees and twenty minutes with the meridian, to a stone standing in the road leading from Bladensburgh to the Eastern Branch Ferry ; then south to a stone eighty poles north of the east and west line, already drawn from the mouth of Goose Creek to the Eastern Branch ; then east, parallel to the said east and west line, to the Eastern Branch ; then with the waters of the Eastern Branch, Potomac River, and Rock Creek, to the beginning,—which has since been called the City of Washington.

The original proprietors, Daniel Carroll, Notley Young, David Burns, and Samuel Davidson, deeded their lands in trust to Thomas Beall and John Mackall Gantt, trustees, who conveyed the same to the Commissioners, and their successors in office, for the United States, forever. The terms of sale are expressed in a letter of March 31, 1791, from the President to the Secretary of State:—

The terms entered into by me, on the part of the United States, with the landholders of Georgetown and Carrollsburgh, are, that all the land from Rock Creek, along the river to the Eastern Branch, and so upwards to or above the Ferry, including a breadth of about a mile and a half, the whole containing from three to five thousand acres, is ceded to the public, on condition that, when the whole shall be surveyed and laid off as a city (which Major L'Enfant is now directed to do), the present proprietors shall retain every other lot; and for such part of the land as may be taken for public use, for squares, walks, &c., they shall be allowed at the rate of $25 per acre,—the public having the right to reserve such parts of the wood on the land as may be thought necessary to be preserved for ornament. The landholders to have the use and profits of the grounds until the city is laid off into lots, and sale is made of those lots, which, by this agreement, become public property. Nothing is to be allowed for the ground which may be occupied for streets and alleys.

Washington's attention was arrested, by the advantages which this location presents for a city, when he was a youthful surveyor of the country around, and he encamped with Braddock's forces on the hill now occupied by the Observatory, which was long known as Camp Hill, from this circumstance. His earnest desire, that the seat of government should be located here, is said also to have had great influence in the decision of Congress. Washington directed Major L'Enfant in planning the city; and, finding him somewhat arbitrary and refractory, he appointed Andrew Ellicott in his place.

In laying out the plan of the city, Mr. Ellicott drew a

meridional line, by astronomical observation, through the area intended for the Capitol, and upon this basis laid off two sets of streets, intersecting each other at right angles, and distinguished by letters and numbers. The streets running north and south are numbered, and those running east and west are lettered, taking the Capitol as a starting point. Avenues were then projected, cutting the streets at various angles, and connecting the most prominent and favorable points of the city,—the avenues intersecting each other and forming open spaces at certain points previously determined upon. These avenues are named after and located to correspond with the position of the different States in the Union, and are from 130 to 160 feet wide; the streets vary from 90 to 110 feet. In the original plan, submitted to Congress in January, 1790, the following improvements were suggested :—

1. An equestrian statue of Washington to occupy the present site of the Washington Monument.

2. An historic and itinerary column to be erected at the intersection of Massachusetts, North Carolina, Kentucky, and Tennessee avenues.

3. A naval column.

4. Squares were to be given to the States for each to improve, and designed for statues, obelisks, etc.

5. A church, for national purposes, to be located where the Patent Office now stands.

6. Five grand fountains, on reservation 17, intersection of F street and Maryland avenue, H street and New York avenue, H street north and Pennsylvania avenue, and Market space.

7. A grand avenue, four hundred feet in breadth, running from the Capitol to the Washington Monument, and

connecting with the President's park, forming a beautiful drive, bordered with gardens and shade trees. In designing this, Major L'Enfant is presumed to have had in mind the garden between the Chamber of Deputies and the Tuileries, at Paris. It was expected that public buildings or residences for the heads of departments and foreign ministers would be erected on this avenue.

8. The water of Tiber Creek was to be conducted to the Capitol, and from thence through the grounds to the canal. In lieu of this supply, a spring of water was conducted to the Capitol from the eastern part of the city.

The city is four miles and a half in length, from northwest to southeast, and two miles and a half in breadth. When the plan was completed, copies were sent to all parts of the country, and to Europe,—an act having been passed allowing aliens to hold lots,—and extensive investments were made. The first speculations in lots proved ruinous, having been engaged in under the supposition that the squares east and south of the Capitol would be taken up immediately; whereas, the location of the public buildings near the President's mansion turned improvement in that direction.

The act of Congress authorizing the removal of the seat of government, required the completion of the public buildings before the first Monday in December, 1800. Washington found the greatest difficulty in procuring sufficient means. The fund donated by Maryland and Virginia was exhausted, and Congress, by act of May 6, 1796, authorized the taking of loans for this purpose. Washington made a personal application to Maryland for a loan of $150,000. The Legislature of Maryland, by resolution of December 22, 1796, granted a loan of

$100,000, on condition of the individual responsibility of the Commissioners. The buildings were reported ready for occupation on the 15th of June, 1800, and during that month the public offices were removed from Philadelphia, and Congress commenced its next session in the City of Washington on the 3d Monday of November following.

It was customary at that time for the President to open the sessions of Congress by an address, delivered in person, instead of sending a message. On this occasion the House of Representatives repaired to the Senate Chamber, after the manner of the British Parliament, and President Adams addressed the two Houses as follows :—

I congratulate the people of the United States on the assembling of Congress at the permanent seat of their government; and I congratulate you, gentlemen, on the prospect of a residence not to be exchanged. It would be unbecoming the Representatives of this nation to assemble for the first time in this solemn temple without looking up to the Supreme Ruler of the universe and imploring His blessing. It is with you, gentlemen, to consider whether the local powers over the District of Columbia, vested by the Constitution in the Congress of the United States, shall be immediately exercised. If, in your opinion, this important trust ought now to be executed, you cannot fail, while performing it, to take into view the future probable situation of the territory, for the happiness of which you are about to provide. You will consider it as the Capital of a great nation, advancing with unexampled rapidity in arts, in commerce, in wealth, and in population, and possessing within itself those resources which, if not thrown away, or lamentably misdirected, will secure to it a long course of prosperity and self-government.

The Senate, in their reply, said : " We meet you, sir, and the other branch of the National Legislature, in the city which is honored by the name of our late hero and sage, the illustrious Washington, with sensations and emotions which exceed our power of description."

The House of Representatives, in reply, said: "The final establishment of the seat of our national government, which has now taken place in the District of Columbia, is an event of no small importance in the political transactions of our country. Nor can we on this occasion omit to express a hope that the spirit which animated the great founder of this city may descend to future generations; and that the wisdom, magnanimity, and steadiness which marked the events of his public life may be imitated in all succeeding ages. A consideration of those powers which have been vested in Congress over the District of Columbia will not escape our attention; nor shall we forget that, in exercising those powers, a regard must be had to those events which will necessarily attend the Capital of America."

The appearance of the city at this time is thus described by the Hon. John Cotton Smith, of Connecticut:—

Our approach to the city was accompanied with sensations not easily described. One wing of the Capitol only had been erected, which, with the President's house, a mile distant from it, both constructed with white sandstone, were shining objects in dismal contrast with the scene around them. Instead of recognizing the avenues and streets portrayed on the plan of the city, not one was visible, unless we except a road, with two buildings on each side of it, called the New Jersey avenue. The Pennsylvania, leading, as laid down on paper, from the Capitol to the Presidential mansion, was then nearly the whole distance a deep morass, covered with alder bushes, which were cut through the width of the intended avenue during the then ensuing Winter. Between the President's house and Georgetown a block of houses had been erected, which then bore, and may still bear, the name of the *six buildings*. There were also two other blocks, consisting of two or three dwelling-houses, in different directions, and now and then an insulated wooden habitation,—the intervening spaces, and indeed the surface of the city generally, being covered with shrub oak bushes on the higher grounds, and on the marshy soil either trees or some sort of shrubbery. Nor was the desolate aspect of the place a little augmented by a number of unfinished edifices at Greenleaf's Point, and on an eminence a short distance from it, commenced by an individual whose name they bore, but the state of whose funds compelled him to abandon them, not only unfinished, but in a ruinous condition. There appeared to be but two really comfortable habitations in all respects within the bounds of the city, one of which belonged to Dudley Carroll, Esq., and the other to Notley Young, who were the former proprietors of a large proportion of the land appropriated to the city, but who reserved for their own accommodation ground sufficient for gardens and other useful appurtenances. The roads in every direction were muddy and unimproved. A sidewalk was attempted in one instance by a covering formed of the chips of the stones which had been hewn for the Capitol. It extended but a little way, and was of little value; for in dry weather the sharp fragments cut our shoes, and in wet weather covered them with white mortar. In short, it was a "new settlement." The houses, with two or three exceptions, had been very recently erected, and the operation greatly hurried in view of the approaching transfer of the national government. A laudable desire was manifested, by what few citizens and residents there were, to render our condition as pleasant as circumstances would permit. One of the blocks of buildings already mentioned was situated on the east side of what was intended for the Capitol square, and, being chiefly occupied by an extensive and well-kept hotel, accommodated a goodly number of the Members. Our little party took lodgings with a Mr. Peacock, in one of the houses on New Jersey avenue, with the addition of Senators Tracy, of Connecticut, and Chipman and Paine, of Vermont; and Representatives Thomas, of Maryland, and Dana, Edmond, and Griswold, of Connecticut. Speaker Sedgwick was allowed a room to himself,—the rest of us

in pairs. To my excellent friend Davenport and myself
was allotted a spacious and decently furnished apartment,
with separate beds, on the lower floor. Our diet was
various, but always substantial, and we were attended by
active and faithful servants. A large proportion of the
southern Members took lodgings at Georgetown, which,
though of a superior order, were three miles distant from
the Capitol, and of course rendered the daily employment
of hackney coaches indispensable.

Notwithstanding the unfavorable aspect which Washington presented on our arrival, I cannot sufficiently express
my admiration of its local position. From the Capitol
you have a distinct view of its fine, undulating surface, situated at the confluence of the Potomac and its Eastern
Branch, the wide expanse of that majestic river to the bend
at Mount Vernon, the cities of Alexandria and Georgetown, and the cultivated fields and blue hills of Maryland
and Virginia on either side of the river, the whole consti-
tuting a prospect of surpassing beauty and grandeur. The
city has also the inestimable advantage of delightful water,
in many instances flowing from copious springs, and always
attainable by digging to a moderate depth; to which may
be added the singular fact that such is the due admixture
of loam and clay in the soil of a great portion of the city
that a house may be built of brick made of the earth dug
from the cellar; hence it was not unusual to see the
remains of a brick-kiln near the newly-erected dwelling-
house or other edifice. In short, when we consider not
only these advantages, but what, in a national point of
view, is of superior importance, the location on a fine,
navigable river, accessible to the whole maritime frontier
of the United States, and yet easily rendered defensible
against foreign invasion,—and that, by the facilities of inter-
nal navigation and railways, it may be approached by the
population of the western States, and indeed of the whole
nation, with less inconvenience than any other conceivable
situation,—we must acknowledge that its selection by Washington as the permanent seat of the federal government affords a striking exhibition of the discernment, wisdom, and

forecast which characterized that illustrious man.   Under
this impression, whenever, during the six years of my connection with Congress, the question of removing the seat of
government to some other place was agitated—and the
proposition was frequently made—I stood almost alone
as a northern man in giving my vote in the negative.

President Adams took possession of the new mansion
on his arrival in November, and Mrs. Adams, in a letter
to her daughter, gave her impressions of the President's
house and the city as follows :—

The house is upon a grand and superb scale, requiring about thirty servants to attend and keep the apartments in proper order, and perform the ordinary business of the house and stables—an establishment very
well proportioned to the President's salary.   The light-
ing the apartments, from the kitchen to parlors and
chambers, is a tax indeed, and the fires we are obliged to
keep to secure us from daily agues is another very cheering
comfort.   To assist us in this great castle, and render less
attendance necessary, bells are wholly wanting, not one
single one being hung through the whole house, and promises are all you can obtain.   This is so great an inconvenience that I know not what to do or how to do.   The
ladies from Georgetown and in the city have many of them
visited me.   Yesterday I returned fifteen visits.   But such
a place as Georgetown appears!   Why, our Milton is
beautiful.   But no comparisons; if they put me up bells,
and let me have wood enough to keep fires, I design *to be
pleased.*   But, surrounded with forests, can you believe
that wood is not to be had, because people cannot be found
to cut and cart it.   *   *   *   *   We have indeed come
into a *new country.*

The house is made habitable, but there is not a single
apartment finished, and all within side, except the plaster-
ing, has been done since B. came.   We have not the *least
fence, yard, or convenience without,* and the great unfinished
audience-room I make a drying-room of, to hang up the

clothes in.   *   *   If the twelve years in which this place has been considered as the future seat of government had been improved, as they would have been in New England, very many of the present inconveniences would have been removed. It is a beautiful spot, capable of any improvement, and the more I view it the more I am delighted with it.

Many amusing jokes were cracked at the expense of the city, in its infancy, by the wags of Philadelphia, New York, and other cities jealous of the location of the seat of government. It was styled the "city of magnificent distances," and the Capitol the "palace in the wilderness." Indeed, the heart of the present city was at that time but waste, swamp, and thicket, and snipe-shooting was common on the borders of Pennsylvania avenue. The Indian name of the place was Conococheague, meaning Roaring Brook, from a stream of that name which falls into the Potomac above Georgetown. The elevated plateau on the east side of the city, known as Capitol Hill, was formerly called Rome by its proprietor, whose name was Pope, and who fancied the title of Pope of Rome. From this circumstance, the inlet from the Potomac was at that time called the Tiber, but the name has since been applied to the small stream emptying into the canal, although General Washington denominated it Goose Creek, in defining the boundary of the city.

Washington was incorporated as a city by act of Congress passed May 3, 1802. Under the auspices of President Jefferson, Pennsylvania avenue was planted with Lombardy poplars, one row on each side and two in the middle, to imitate the beautiful walk and drive in Berlin, known as Unter den Linden. The poplars, however, did not flourish, and were removed when the avenue was graded and paved, by acts of Congress passed May 25, 1832, and February 19, 1833. The city was planned on a grand, national scale, too extensive for municipal improvement alone, and Congress originally proposed to make liberal expenditures in adorning the squares, grading streets and avenues, and decorating public buildings and grounds in a manner becoming the court city of a nation. Congress has not displayed a proper spirit under the circumstances, and has never appropriated funds equal to a tax upon the government property in the city.

Frequent attempts have been made to remove the seat of government, but public sentiment has been uniformly opposed to it, although the constitutionality of a removal is conceded.

BRITISH CAPTURE OF WASHINGTON.

In the Spring of the year 1814 some apprehensions were felt, by the administration at Washington, of an attack upon the seat of government, by British forces from Admiral Cockburn's fleet, then ravaging the coasts of Maryland and Virginia, and the shores of the Chesapeake. Apprisals of the danger were sent to this government from our ministers abroad, and, in view of this, President Madison immediately ordered a militia organization sufficient for such an emergency. In order to check the inroads of Cockburn's fleet, a flotilla of barges, carrying heavy guns, was fitted out and put under the command of Captain Joshua Barney, an experienced privateersman, who succeeded in eluding the pursuit of the British fleet, while he did the enemy much injury, and kept them from making further spoliations. The alarm of intended invasion was treated with contempt by John Armstrong, the

4

Secretary of War, and the *National Intelligencer*, then the leading journal. General Armstrong sneered at the probability of an attempt to plunder the Sheep-Walk, as he styled the federal city, of eight thousand inhabitants, with streets scarcely defined by foot-paths.

Admiral Cochrane sailed from Bermuda, on the 3d of August, with three thousand troops, under Major-General Robert Ross, and arrived in the Chesapeake on the 14th, where he joined Cockburn's fleet, making in all twenty sail. This fleet sailed up the bay and debarked four thousand troops, under General Ross and Admiral Cockburn, at Benedict, on the left bank of the Patuxent River, on the 20th of August. On the afternoon of the 21st the little army set out on the march for Washington, without artillery or cavalry, and, after a trying march under a broiling sun, which caused many to sink from fatigue, the town of Bladensburgh was reached, on the 24th of August, without the slightest molestation.

By order of William Jones, Secretary of the Navy, the Barney flotilla was blown up at 9 in the morning of the 22d,—and the sound of the explosion cheered up the enemy on what their commander considered a desperate undertaking. The approach of the British, under Ross and Cockburn, had been ascertained and observed by President Madison in person, and he attended eight thousand undisciplined militia to the heights of Bladensburgh to meet them. Our forces were placed under the command of General Winder, and consisted mainly of raw militia ordered out for the occasion. Captain Barney, with four hundred seamen and some field pieces, joined the army of defence immediately after giving orders for the destruction of his flotilla. The British opened a fire upon our lines about one o'clock in the afternoon of the 24th, and their advances were promptly checked by a terribly-destructive fire from Barney's artillery, which kept its position until four o'clock, while the militia under the command of General Winder seem to have been kept out of musket range.   It is a remarkable fact that the militia met with little or no loss, notwithstanding the engagement continued for three hours, and each of the enemy was supplied with sixty rounds of ball cartridges. The fighting was done entirely by the seamen under Commodore Barney,—for, upon the first charge received by the militia, they broke and fell back, and finally fled altogether, leaving Barney unsupported.   He was soon flanked by superior numbers, and fell, wounded, among eleven of his marines, who were killed by his side.   Captain Barney ordered his men to retreat, and surrendered himself to a British officer.   The conduct of the militia was extremely disgraceful, and any attempt to exonerate the retreat would be to stigmatize the American character and arms with cowardice.   Our raw recruits never behaved so badly before or since.   General Winder was loth to expose the citizens of Washington and Baltimore, who composed the ranks, to destruction by British regulars,—and the militia-men, partaking naturally of the same spirit, took to their heels and fled into the woods without waiting for their prudent General to sound a retreat.   The seamen under Barney received the highest commendation from the British, on the field.   The facts in the case are stated by Gleig, an officer of the 85th Royal regiment, on duty on this occasion :—

This battle, by which the fate of the American Capitol was decided, began about one o'clock in the afternoon, and lasted till four. The loss on the part of the English was severe, since, out of two-thirds of the army, which were engaged, upwards of five hundred men were killed and wounded; and what rendered it doubly severe was, that among these were numbered several officers of rank and distinction. Colonel Thornton, who commanded the light brigade; Lieutenant-Colonel Wood, commanding the 85th regiment; and Major Brown, who had led the advanced guard, were all severely wounded; and General Ross himself had a horse shot under him. On the side of the Americans the slaughter was not so great. Being in possession of a strong position, they were of course less exposed in defending, than the others in storming it; and had they conducted themselves with coolness and resolution, it is not conceivable how the day could have been won. But the fact is, that, with the exception of a party of sailors from the gun boats, under the command of Commodore Barney, no troops could behave worse than they did. The skirmishers were driven in as soon as attacked, the first line gave way without offering the slightest resistance, and the left of the main body was broken within half an hour after it was seriously engaged. Of the sailors, however, it would be injustice not to speak in the terms which their conduct merits. They were employed as gunners, and not only did they serve their guns with a quickness and precision which astonished their assailants, but they stood till some of them were actually bayoneted with fuses in their hands; nor was it till their leader was wounded and taken, and they saw themselves deserted on all sides by the soldiers, that they quitted the field.

It must be remarked that Gleig's statement of the loss of the British refers to the number of killed, wounded, missing, and deserters, from the morning of the battle until their re-embarkation, including the casualties in Washington. Ross, in his dispatch, dated August 30th, stated the loss in the action at Bladensburgh to be sixty-four killed, and one hundred and eighty-five wounded and missing.

On the other hand, the citizen militia escaped, pretty much unhurt, with their valuable lives; and without forming again to impede the progress of the enemy, or to defend the Capitol and public buildings, disappeared entirely from the District, leaving their wives and families to the mercy of the victors.

The third British brigade was led into the city by General Ross, and marshaled in front of the Capitol. In approaching the Capitol the horse of General Ross was shot under him by one of Barney's sailors, who had ensconced himself in a house for that purpose. The inmates of the house were immediately put to the sword and the house set in flames. A volley was fired into the windows of the Capitol, when the soldiers entered and prepared its destruction. Admiral Cockburn mounted the Speaker's chair, and put the question, "Shall this harbor of Yankee democracy be burned? All for it will say aye!" After reversing the question, he pronounced the motion carried unanimously, and ordered combustibles to be applied to the furniture. In a room adjoining the Senate chamber portraits of Louis the Sixteenth and Marie Antoinette, King and Queen of France, were cut out of the frames and burned or stolen. The building was fired in several places and soon wrapped in flames.

The Secretary of the Navy had previously given orders to Commodore Tingey to destroy the shipping and stores at the Navy Yard, in the event of a defeat at Bladensburgh, to prevent their falling into the hands of the enemy.

At four o'clock the Secretary of War dispatched a messenger to Tingey, informing him that no further protection could be expected,—upon which that officer pre- . pared to fire the vessels and buildings. Earnest appeals were made by the citizens, and even the ladies, to save the yard from destruction, but without avail. At twenty minutes past eight o'clock the match was applied to the train, and the work of the enemy was performed by our own hands. The sloop-of-war Argus with ten guns mounted, five barges fully armed, two gun-boats, the frigate Columbia on the stocks, and a large quantity of naval stores, were consigned to the flames. The schooner Lynx, and the Arsenal, by some oversight, escaped the sacrifice.

The scene is thus described by Lieutenant Gleig, as it appeared to the British on entering the city :—

While the third brigade was thus employed, the rest of the army, having recalled its stragglers and removed the wounded into Bladensburgh, began its march towards Washington. Though the battle was ended by four o'clock, the sun had set before the different regiments were in a condition to move, consequently this short journey was performed in the dark. The work of destruction had also begun in the city before they quitted their ground, and the blazing of houses, ships, and stores—the report of exploding magazines and the crash of falling roofs—informed them as they proceeded of what was going forward. You can conceive nothing finer than the sight which met them as they drew near to the town. The sky was brilliantly illuminated by the different conflagrations, and a dark-red light was thrown upon the road, sufficient to permit each man to view distinctly his comrade's face. Except the burning of St. Sebastian's, I do not recollect to have witnessed at any period of my life a scene more striking or more sublime. Having advanced as far as the plain where the reserve had previously paused, the first and second brigades halted, and, forming into close column, passed the night in bivouac.

After firing the Capitol, the British commanders took their silent march to the other end of Pennsylvania avenue, and having taken possession of the lodging-house of Mrs. Suter, opposite the Treasury Department, they ordered supper. Meanwhile they set fire to the Treasury building and the President's Mansion. The President had retired from the city with his Cabinet, on horseback, immediately after the close of the battle at Bladensburgh, —crossing the Potomac at the Little Falls, re-crossing at the Great Falls, and returning after the evacuation by the enemy.

It is stated by Gleig that the table was found spread at the President's House, and covers laid for forty guests, in view of a welcome of the victorious defenders of the city. The wine was cooling on the sideboard, the plates warming at the grate, and meats on the spits in the kitchen, ready for a sumptuous repast. However, no repast was enjoyed by the hostile troops, as Ross and Cockburn returned to the house of Mrs. Suter, and, after extinguishing the lights, ate their supper by the blaze of the burning buildings.

Later in the evening General Ross rejoined the main army at their encampment on Capitol Hill, when they were exposed to the inclemency of a severe thunder storm which occurred in the night. Admiral Cockburn, with a few of his dissolute companions, spent the night in a brothel, rivaling the elements in rendering the night hideous with their disgusting orgies. During the night the sentries were attacked, in a fit of rashness, by a grand-nephew of General Washington—John Lewis, a young sailor. He was shot down in the street, where he was found dead in the morning. The Long Bridge across the

Potomac was fired simultaneously, at both ends, by the British and Americans, under the false apprehension of an attack from the opposite shore. In its destruction some military stores were burned upon the Virginia side.

On the morning of the 25th the two commanders renewed their work of demolition by burning the building occupied by the War and Navy Departments. Cockburn, mounted upon a switch-tailed mare, and followed by her foal, paraded the streets, enjoying the effect of his ludicrous appearance and the terror of the women and children. The Post and Patent Office was, with reluctance, spared by the enemy, upon the appeal of Dr. Thornton, to save private property stored in the building.

Cockburn took personal revenge upon the editors of the *National Intelligencer*, for some remarks published concerning him, by destroying the presses in the office and throwing the type out of the windows,—the Admiral enjoining upon them to "be sure that all the C's were destroyed, that the rascals could have no further means of abusing his name," and declaring that "he would punish Madison's man, Joe, as he had his master, Jim." That venerable sheet, in its usual conservative spirit, a few days afterwards attributed the acts of plunder entirely to lawless citizens. This article was the basis of the statement, in a London journal, that "the only acts of robbery and destruction of private property were admitted to have been perpetrated by our own countrymen!" Besides the destruction of private property already mentioned, the houses of General Washington and Mr. Frost, and the hotel of Daniel Carroll, were burned on Capitol Hill.

The destroyers then proceeded to the Navy Yard to complete the ruin in which they had been too promptly anticipated. Not content with burning the public works and stores, they also set fire to the private rope-walks of Tench, Ringgold, Heath & Co., and John Chalmers, and shamefully mutilated the beautiful monument erected by the officers of the navy to the gallant heroes who fell, at Tripoli, in a war to secure British as well as American rights, and to punish pirates, the enemies of mankind.

After setting fire to the rope-walks on Greenleaf's Point, the torch was thrown into a dry well, in which the Americans had previously cast a large quantity of powder, arms, and military stores. The consequence was a tremendous explosion, which brought death and destruction upon all around. Nearly one hundred of the barbarous invaders were killed and wounded, and their mutilated remains scattered in every direction.

In addition to the general consternation produced by this casualty, a frightful tornado swept over the city, which threw down buildings and dealt destruction to everything in its path. The blackness of the sky, the howling of the tempest, the cataract of rain, the gleaming of the lightning, the roar of thunder, and the crash of falling buildings, conspired to render the scene terrific beyond description, striking terror to the hearts of friend and foe. Trees were torn up by the roots, and roofs of houses whirled in the air like sheets of paper. Scores of the enemy, as well as inhabitants, were buried amid the ruins of fallen buildings, and the elements seemed to unite in completing the work of the despoilers. The British now taking a needless alarm for their own safety, falsely apprehending an attack, withdrew stealthily from the city, as the evening closed in, and took up their march for the point of embarkation.

4*

CHAPTER III.

EXECUTIVE DEPARTMENTS OF THE GOVERNMENT.

BEFORE entering upon a description of the departments of the government, we have some pride and much pleasure in stating that any individual having legitimate business with any department, from the President downwards, will find that all reasonable requests are met with the utmost politeness. From the highest to the lowest, the conduct of the officials at the seat of government is regulated by a code of courtesy which is based upon the recognized sovereignty of the people. No fees are needed to procure access to the President or the chiefs of departments during the hours set apart for the approach of the public. If a document has been filed away in some dusty pigeon-hole for half a century, and you are entitled to peruse it, although it may require several days of labor, the proper officer will in due time produce it for your inspection. No armed sentinels morosely oppose the entrance of the humblest; patience seems to be the universal characteristic of the employes. Perhaps it may not be out of place to suggest that an equal courtesy requires the visitor to avoid an unnecessary consumption of public time by requesting what cannot be given, or asking questions which cannot be answered.

THE EXECUTIVE MANSION AND THE PRESIDENT.

The Executive Mansion, generally known as the "White House," is situated in the western portion of the city, surrounded by the War, Navy, Treasury, and State Departments. The building was commenced in 1792, and was modeled after the palace of the Duke of Leinster. A premium for the best design having been offered by the Commissioners of the City of Washington, James Hoban presented a plan, which was accepted. On the 13th of October, 1792, a procession was formed, and the corner-stone was laid with due formality. The building is one hundred and seventy feet front and eighty-six deep; it is built of freestone, painted white, with Ionic pilasters, comprehending two lofty stories of rooms, crowned with a balustrade. The north front is ornamented with a portico, of four Ionic columns in front, and a projecting screen with three columns. The outer intercolumniation is for carriages; the middle space is the entrance for visitors who come on foot; the steps from both lead to a broad platform in front of the door of entrance. The garden front is varied by having a rusticated basement story under the Ionic ordonnance, and by a semicircular projecting colonnade of six columns, with two flights of steps leading from the ground to the level of the principal story. In the interior, the north entrance opens immediately into a spacious hall of forty by fifty feet. Advancing through a screen of Ionic columns, apparently of white marble, but only an imitation, the door in the centre opens into the oval room, or saloon, of forty by thirty feet. Adjoining this room are two others, each thirty by twenty-two feet in size; these form a suite of apartments devoted to occasions of ceremony. The great banqueting-room occupies the whole depth of the east side of the mansion, and is eighty feet long by forty feet wide, with a clear height of twenty-two feet. Inadequate as the building is now confessed to be for the accommodation of the chief magistrate of the nation, there was a time when it was deemed quite too extensive and grand, as is evident by the following extract from the correspondence of Oliver Wolcott, under date of July 4, 1800: "It was built to be looked at by visitors and strangers, and will render its occupant an object of ridicule with some and of pity with others. It must be cold and damp in Winter, and cannot be kept in tolerable order without a regiment of servants."

Notwithstanding this prophetic declaration, in which there is much of truth, time has demonstrated that, despite all the risks of cold, damp, ridicule, and pity, a tenant has always been found willing to venture the dangers of its occupancy. As indicated in Chapter II., the Executive Mansion was injured during the British invasion; in 1815 it was repaired, under the superintendence of James Hoban. So unfit is the mansion for the purpose to which it is devoted that the Commissioner of Public Buildings has frequently called the attention of Congress to the fact, and, in 1860, felt obliged to use the following plain but emphatic terms:—

Much has been done to the President's House in the way of repairs. The roof requires constant attention and expenditure of money. The copper was not put on properly. The sheets simply lap, instead of being grooved, and consequently the temperature acting upon the copper, alternately contracting and expanding it, opens the seams and produces leaks which disfigure and greatly injure the ceilings. To repair it as it ought to be would cost almost as much as a new roof. The house is now in as good order as it can be made, with the temporary repairs that are usually put upon it. Unless thoroughly renovated, owing to its age, it will soon again be out of repair. It is almost impossible to keep such an old building in a habitable condition.

A fine conservatory and green-house are connected with the house, and the grounds adjacent are well kept and tastefully laid out. Looking southward, the view of the Potomac River is very beautiful, and during the Summer a fountain gratifies the eye and soothes the ear with its ripplings.

In the lawn, on the north side, is a bronze statue of Jefferson, the ownership of which is somewhat doubtful, as it was purchased by Capt. Levy, U. S. N., and offered to, but not accepted by, the Senate of the United States.

The President.—In other portions of this volume, as the reader will perceive by referring to the index, we have indicated the mode of election, tenure of office, salary and duties of the President; in the chapter upon etiquette, we have also explained the laws of courtesy governing the citizen in his approach to the elected chief of the government. It only remains therefore to announce that, while the President is a public servant, he is not the servant of each individual composing that mythical tyranny, "The Public." Let it be understood that while every man who becomes President of the United States agrees to devote certain portions of certain days to miscellaneous hand-shakings and applications for opportunities to serve the republic, *his time is very precious,* and no one individual, unless charged with most extraordinary public business, is entitled to more than two minutes of conversation with him.

The inauguration of the President usually, but not necessarily, takes place in Washington. The Constitution provides for the election of President by the observance of the following forms :—

1. He must be a native-born citizen, or a citizen of the United States at the time of the adoption of the Constitution, and must have attained the age of thirty-five years; and, from the commencement of the government, so wisely was this requirement conceived, that no person under the age of forty years has filled the presidential chair.

2. Congress may determine the time of choosing the electors, and the day on which they shall give their votes, which day shall be the same throughout the United States.

3. Each State shall appoint, in such manner as the Legislature thereof may direct, a number of electors, equal to the whole number of Senators and Representatives to which the State may be entitled in the Congress; but no Senator, or Representative, or person holding an office of trust or profit under the United States, shall be appointed an elector. The electors shall meet in their respective States, and vote by ballot for President and Vice-President, one of whom, at least, shall not be an inhabitant of the same State with themselves; they shall name in their ballots the person voted for as President, and in distinct ballots the person voted for as Vice-President; and they shall make distinct lists of all persons voted for as President, and all persons voted for as Vice-President, and of the number of votes for each, which lists they shall sign and certify, and transmit, sealed, to the seat of the government of the United States, directed to the President of the

Senate. The President of the Senate shall, in the presence of the Senate and House of Representatives, open all the certificates, and the votes shall then be counted; the person having the greatest number of votes for President shall be the President, if such number be a majority of the whole number of electors appointed; and if no person have such majority, then, from the persons having the highest numbers, not exceeding three, on the list of those voted for as President, the House of Representatives shall choose immediately, by ballot, the President. But in choosing the President, the votes shall be taken by States, the representation from each State having one vote; a quorum for this purpose, to consist of a member or members from two-thirds of the States, and a majority of all the States shall be necessary to a choice; and if the House of Representatives shall not choose a President, whenever the right of choice shall devolve upon them, before the fourth day of March next following, then the Vice-President, elected by the Senate, shall act as President, as in the case of the death or other constitutional disability of the President. The person having the greatest number of votes as Vice-President shall be the Vice-President, if such number be a majority of the whole number of electors appointed; and if no person have a majority, then, from the two highest numbers on the list, the Senate shall choose the Vice-President; a quorum for the purpose shall consist of two-thirds of the whole number of Senators, and a majority of the whole number shall be necessary to a choice. But no person constitutionally ineligible to the office of President shall be eligible to that of Vice-President of the United States.

There are certain hours of every day, except the days

of Cabinet meetings, usually from 11 until 1 o'clock, during which the President may properly be approached either upon business or with the intention simply to pay him respect.

Inauguration of the President.—The Constitution of the United States prescribes no form for the installation of the Chief Executive into the duties of his office; it only requires of him that, before he enters on the execution of his duties, he shall take the following oath or affirmation: " I do solemnly swear (or affirm) that I will faithfully execute the office of President of the United States, and will, to the best of my ability, preserve, protect, and defend the Constitution of the United States." There is no law specifying where this oath or affirmation shall be taken, and it would be equally valid if attested by a village magistrate or the Chief Justice of the Supreme Court of the United States. Each incumbent of the office, therefore, has been governed by the dictates of his own fancy or judgment in the ceremonies attending his induction.

Thus, when George Washington was first inaugurated President, on the 1st of May, 1789, he was escorted from his house to the city hall, where the custom-house has since been erected, in Wall street, New York, and the oath of office was administered to him by Chancellor Livingston. After his re-election, in 1793, delegations from the Senate and House of Representatives, with other dignitaries, assembled in the Senate chamber to witness the renewal of General Washington's oath. John Adams, in 1797, informed the Senate and House of Representatives of his election to the office of President of the United States, and of his readiness to take the constitutional oath. On the 4th of March, at noon, he took his seat in the chair of the Speaker of the House of Representatives, and, after delivering an inaugural address, took the oath of office and retired. On the 2d of March, 1801, Thomas Jefferson informed the Speaker of the House of Representatives of his intention to take the oath of office in the Senate chamber, on the 4th day of the same month, at noon. He also delivered an inaugural address, and was the first President whose inauguration took place in Washington. Upon the re-election of Jefferson, he omitted the address, and assumed his oath in the presence of Chief Justice Marshall and Justices Cushing, Patterson, and Washington, of the Supreme Court; and it is stated that amongst the distinguished witnesses was the gallant Commodore Preble. On the 4th of March, 1809, James Madison, who had been Secretary of State during the two terms of Jefferson's administration, took the oath of office, after delivering his inaugural address, in the chamber of the House of Representatives. Having been re-elected, he appeared at the Capitol on the 4th of March, 1813, and, after delivering his second inaugural address, he was sworn into office by Chief Justice Marshall. The first time that a public address, outside the Capitol, was delivered, was when, in 1817, James Monroe was inducted into the presidential honors and responsibilities. On that occasion the Vice-President was first sworn in; the President then, from an elevated platform, pronounced his inaugural address, took the oath in the presence of the Chief Justice of the Supreme Court, and, after a salute of artillery, retired to the Executive Mansion. On the 4th of March, 1821, President Monroe having been re-elected, could not be sworn into office,—that date happening to fall upon Sunday, *dies non* in law. On the following day, however—Monday, the 5th of March, a very inclement day—the oath was again administered by Chief Justice Marshall. The next President was John Quincy Adams, who, at twenty minutes after 12 o'clock of the 4th day of March, 1825, placed himself in the chair of the Speaker of the House of Representatives, and having delivered an address, which occupied about three quarters of an hour, he read, from a copy of the laws of the United States, handed to him by the Chief Justice of the Supreme Court, the appointed obligation. This ceremony having been performed, he received the congratulations of those present, including General Andrew Jackson, and with proper formalities and an escort was conducted to the Executive Mansion. Andrew Jackson was inducted into the presidency on the 4th of March, 1829. The Vice-President, John C. Calhoun, having passed through the necessary preliminaries, assumed his seat as President of the Senate, at eleven o'clock of the above-named day. Precisely at twelve o'clock General Jackson commenced the delivery of his inaugural address, standing upon the eastern portico of the Capitol, and in presence of an immense concourse of people. At the conclusion of the discourse, Chief Justice Marshall administered the oath of office prescribed by the Constitution. Jackson was again installed President of the United States on the 4th of March, 1833,—Martin Van Buren having been chosen by the people for Vice-President. On this occasion Jackson delivered an address and took the oath of office in the hall of the House of Representatives. Martin Van Buren, having served during four years as the Vice-President under Jackson, was, on the 4th of March, 1837, inducted into the presidential office. The Vice-President was sworn into his office, and, having made a brief speech, assumed his position as President of the Senate. At twelve o'clock Van Buren, accompanied by Jackson, repaired to the Senate chamber, and from thence to the east portico, where, the former having pronounced his address in the presence of an immense multitude, amongst whom Webster and Clay were conspicuous, the oath of office was administered by Chief Justice Taney. The remarkable episode in the political history of the United States, detailed in the records of 1840, resulted in the election of William H. Harrison, who was inaugurated into his office on Friday, the 4th of March, 1841. General Harrison proceeded from his quarters to the Capitol, mounted upon a white charger, and surrounded by an enthusiastic throng of friends. In the Senate chamber, Mr. Tyler having taken the oath of Vice-President, delivered an address. At twenty minutes after twelve General Harrison was ushered in, after which the assemblage proceeded to the eastern portico, where the President delivered the greater portion of his address, and, having received the obligation of office from the Chief Justice, finished his speech, and, under escort, took possession of the Executive Mansion.

The presidency of General Harrison, like that of Taylor, was of brief duration, for, on the 4th of April, 1841, one month from the date of his installation, he died, and the duties and responsibilities of the position devolved upon the Vice-President, John Tyler, who, upon the 6th of April, appeared before the Chief Judge of the Circuit Court, and, for prudential reasons, assumed the presidential oath,—Judge Cranch recording the fact in the following form :—

DISTRICT OF COLUMBIA,   } ss.
City and County of Washington.

I, William Cranch, Chief Judge of the Circuit Court of the District of Columbia, certify that the above-named John Tyler personally appeared before me this day, and although he deems himself qualified to perform the duties and exercise the powers and office of President, on the death of W. H. Harrison, late President of the United States, and without any other oath than that which he has taken as Vice-President, yet, as doubts may arise, and for greater caution, took and subscribed the foregoing before me.

April 6, 1841.   W. CRANCH.

President Tyler having served his term of office, was succeeded, in 1845, by James K. Polk, at whose inauguration the "Empire Club," at that time an imposing political organization in the city of New York, occupied a very conspicuous place in the procession. Mr. Dallas, the Vice-President, having taken his oath, assumed the presidential chair of the Senate and delivered a brief inaugural, after which, Mr. Tyler and Mr. Polk having been ushered into the Senate chamber, the President elect, accompanied by his escort, proceeded to the eastern portico, where, having read his address, Mr. Polk was sworn into office by the Chief Justice, after which the President held a levee at the Executive Mansion. In 1848 Zachary Taylor was elected President of the United States, and Millard Fillmore Vice-President. The 4th of March again falling upon a Sunday, the inauguration was postponed until Monday,—so that in the history of the United States there have been two days when we have had no President, and yet the wheels of government have observed their appointed revolutions.

General Taylor, prior to his installation, had chosen Willards' hotel (since greatly enlarged) for his temporary residence, and, from his lodgings there, was conducted to the Senate, where the obligation of office had been previously administered to the Vice-President elect. In a few minutes the Senate chamber was vacated, and the assemblage proceeded to the eastern portico of the Capitol, from which, like most of his predecessors, General Taylor pronounced an address, after which the oath of office was administered by Chief Justice Taney.

President Taylor died July 9th, 1850, and, in accordance with the Constitution, Millard Fillmore became his successor. On Thursday, July 11th, 1850, Mr. Fillmore appeared before the House of Representatives, and having taken the presidential oath became the President of the United States, and filled that high position up to the 4th of March, 1853, when he was succeeded by Franklin Pierce, who, from Willards' hotel, was accompanied by Mr. Fillmore, Hon. Jesse D. Bright and Hon. Hannibal Hamlin as a committee of Congress, and escorted by a company of U. S. flying artillery, a company of U. S. marines, and seventeen volunteer military companies. Arriving at the Capitol, Mr. Pierce took his oath of office on the east portico, and having delivered an address, without using manuscript, he went to the Executive Mansion where he held a public levee. James Buchanan was installed into his office March 4th, 1857. He was the fifteenth President of the United States; and, like several of his predecessors, selected Willards' hotel for his temporary residence. From his lodgings he was escorted to the Senate chamber, in the Capitol, where the oath was administered to him by the Hon. James M. Mason, of Virginia, President *pro tem.*, after which, Mr. Breckinridge having made a short address, the whole assemblage proceeded to the east portico, from the platform of which Mr. Buchanan delivered his inaugural to an enthusiastic auditory. In 1860 Abraham Lincoln and Hannibal Hamlin were indicated, by the popular vote and the electoral college, as the proper persons for the respective offices of President and Vice-President during the succeeding term. The inauguration takes place March 4th, 1861.

DEPARTMENT OF STATE.

To the student of American history there is no more interesting or encouraging field of research than is contained in the progressive development of the various executive departments of the government. At first the duties were fully discharged by one or two clerks, but in seventy years the same duties have so multiplied as to require a small army of officials to perform them, and immense palaces for their accommodation. The building devoted to the department now under consideration is situated on Fifteenth street; it will soon be replaced by the magnificent structure which is known as the "Treasury Extension." The plans for this extension were designed by Mr. T. U. Walter, and were accepted by Congress. It was thought best to depart from a strict architectural uniformity with the old portion, and by an ingenious device the new building was so far isolated from the old as to give an opportunity for a correction of the defective details of the former edifice. When completed, the building will be 465 feet long by 266 wide, with four fronts on as many streets; and the interior space will be subdivided, by a centre building, into two courts, each 130 feet square.

The history of the State Department of the United States commences in July, 1789, at which time the first Congress enacted a law entitled " An act for establishing an executive department of the government, to be denominated the Department of Foreign Affairs." By this law, an officer was to be appointed as Secretary for the Department of Foreign Affairs, whose duties were to be performed conformably *to the instructions of the President*. Before this, while the republic was struggling for the recognition of the great nations, its foreign affairs were conducted through commissioners appointed by Congress. Shortly before the adoption of the Constitution, the necessity for some organization of our diplomatic correspondence led to the passage of a resolution of Congress authorizing the appointment of a Secretary of Foreign Affairs. His powers were derived from Congress, and he was required to hold himself amenable to that body, to attend its sessions, and to report and explain all matters pertaining to his province. In September, 1789, another act of Congress changed the designation of the department to that of " Department of State," and defined additional duties to be performed by the " Secretary of State." The rise and progress of American diplomacy, as exhibited in its organization, furnishes a theme from which we turn with reluctance. But the following episode in its history, preserved in the comprehensive pages of Ingersoll's " Historical Sketch of the Second War of the United States," is too creditable to the department and too honorable to its faithful servants to be omitted :—

The day before the fall of Washington—a day of extreme alarm—on the 23d of August, 1814, the Secretary of State wrote to the President: "The enemy are advanced six miles on the road to the wood-yard, and our troops retreating; our troops on the march to meet them, but in too small a body to engage; General Winder proposes to retire till he can collect them in a body. The enemy are in full march for Washington, and have the materials prepared to destroy the bridge.—Tuesday, nine o'clock. You had better remove the records." Before that note was received, Mr. John Graham, chief clerk in the Department of State, and another clerk, Mr. Stephen Pleasanton, bestirred themselves to save the precious public records of that department. The clerk then in charge of most of those archives was Josiah King, who accompanied the government from Philadelphia to Washington. By the exertions of these clerks, principally Mr. Pleasanton, coarse linen bags were purchased, enough to contain the papers. The original Declaration of Independence, the articles of confederation, the federal Constitution, many treaties and laws as enrolled, General Washington's commission as commander-in-chief of the army of the Revolution, which he relinquished when he resigned it at Annapolis (found among the rubbish of a garret), together with many other papers, the loss of which would have deeply blackened our disgrace, and, deposited in the Tower at London, as much illustrated the British triumph—all were carefully secured in linen bags, hung round the room, ready, at a moment's warning, for removal to some place of safety. Wagons, carts, and vehicles of all sorts were in such demand for the army, whose officers took the right of seizing them, whenever necessary, to carry their baggage, provisions, and other conveniences, that it was difficult to procure one in which to load the documents. That done, however, Mr. Pleasanton took them to a mill,

over the Potomac, about three miles beyond Georgetown, where they were concealed. But, as General Mason's cannon-foundry was not far from the mill, though on the Maryland side of the river, apprehension arose that the cannon-foundry, which the enemy would of course seek to destroy, might bring them too near the mill, and endanger its deposits. They were, therefore, removed as far as Leesburg, a small town in Virginia, thirty-five miles from Washington, whither Mr. Pleasanton, on horseback, accompanied the wagon during the battle of Bladensburg. From Leesburg, where he slept that night, the burning city was discernible, in whose blaze the fate of his charge, if left there, was told on the horizon.   *   *   *   *
*   *   *   Mr. Pleasanton took them [the papers] in several carts to the mill, where the carts were discharged; he slept at the Rev. Mr. Maffit's, two miles from the mill, and next morning got country wagons in which he, on horseback, attended the papers to Leesburg, where they were put in a vacant stone house prepared for him by the Rev. Mr. Littlejohn. That fearful night was followed by next day's tornado, which at Leesburg, as at Washington, uprooted trees, unroofed tenements, and everywhere around superadded tempestuous to belligerent destruction and alarm.

Many of the records of the War, Treasury and Navy Departments were destroyed; some were saved, less by any care than by the tempest which arrested hostile destruction before its completion, and drove the enemy from the capital. After their departure several of the written books of the departments were found in the mud, soaked with water from the rain which so opportunely fell,—which, by drying them in the sun and rebinding them, were recovered. Great numbers of books and papers, however, were irrecoverably lost.

The organization of the Department of State embraces the Secretary of State, Assistant Secretary of State, Chief Clerk, Superintendent of Statistics, Translator, Librarian, and twenty-two clerks, who, for the systematic discharge

5

of their official duties, are divided into the following
bureaus :—

The Diplomatic Branch, which has charge of all correspondence between the department and other diplomatic agents of the United States abroad, and those of
foreign powers accredited to this government. In it all
diplomatic instructions sent from the department, and
communications to commissioners under treaties of boundaries, &c., are prepared, copied, and recorded ; and all of
like character received are registered and filed, their contents being first entered in an analytic table or index.

The Consular Branch, which has charge of the correspondence between the department and the consuls
and commercial agents of the United States. In it instructions to those officers, and answers to their dispatches,
and to letters from other persons asking for consular
agencies, or relating to consular affairs are prepared and
recorded.

The Disbursing Agent, who has charge of all correspondence and other matters connected with accounts
relating to any fund with the disbursement of which the
department is charged.

The Translator, whose duties are to furnish such trans-
lations as the department may require. He also records
the commissions of consuls and vice-consuls, when not in
English, upon which exequaturs are issued.

The Clerk of Appointments and Commissions makes
out and records commissions, letters of appointment, and
nominations to the Senate ; makes out and records exequaturs, and records, when in English, the commissions
on which they are issued. He also has charge of the
library.

The Clerk of the Rolls and Archives takes charge of the rolls, or enrolled acts and resolutions of Congress, as they are received at the department from the President; prepares the authenticated copies thereof which are called for; prepares for, and superintends their publication, and that of treaties, in the newspapers and in book form; attends to their distribution throughout the United States, and that of all documents and publications in regard to which this duty is assigned to the department, writing and answering all letters connected therewith. Has charge of all Indian treaties, and business relating thereto.

The Clerk of Territorial Business has charge of the seals of the United States and of the department, and prepares and attaches certificates to papers presented for authentication; has charge of the territorial business; immigration and registered seamen; records all letters from the department, other than the diplomatic and consular.

The Clerk of Pardons and Passports prepares and records pardons and remissions, and registers and files the petitions and papers on which they are founded; makes out and records passports; keeps a daily register of all letters, other than diplomatic and consular, received, and of the disposition made of them; prepares letters relating to this business.

The Superintendent of Statistics prepares the "Annual Report of the Secretary of State and Foreign Commerce," as required by the acts of 1842 and 1856.

The State Department is the official channel through which the government is addressed by the accredited agents of the following foreign powers: By Envoys Extraordinary and Ministers Plenipotentiary, from Belgium,

Brazil, Costa Rica, France, Great Britain, Guatimala, Mexico, New Granada, Portugal, Prussia, Russia, and Spain; by Ministers Resident, from Austria, Bremen, Netherlands, Peru, Sweden, Denmark, Sardinia, and Switzerland. With two or three unimportant exceptions. the Foreign Ministers reside in Washington.

The library contains a very fine collection of books, and, with the many important documents in the keeping of the department, is worthy of examination.

TREASURY DEPARTMENT.

In the first session of the first Congress, an act was passed, which was approved on the second day of September, 1789, to " Establish the Treasury Department." By this legislation, a Secretary, Comptroller, Solicitor, Treasurer, and Assistant Secretary were ordered to be appointed.

The walls of the Treasury extension, above the cellar, are : a basement story, forming a stylobate, and, resting on it, an ordonnance of antæ, of the Ionic order, 45 feet in height. The stylobate is intended to be decidedly of a Grecian character; its base, die, and cornice are beautiful in themselves, but as here brought together they have an effect peculiarly appropriate and pleasing. The window openings in the die are managed so as to give them all the character needed, without loading them with ornament; and the whole arrangement of sills and piers, and the continued cornice, which serves as a window cap, is entirely novel. The antæ and the filling of the spaces between them are so arranged as to accomplish the very difficult combination of the adaptation of Grecian architecture to modern uses, without spoiling its inherent beauties. The style of architecture is more fully preserved, and its design carried out, by the use of single blocks for the columns and antæ. The arrangement of the interior of the new building varies essentially from that of the old, and from public offices generally, in being divided into larger and more commodious rooms. Instead of the narrow, cell-like apartments, with one, or at most two, windows, into which the public departments in Washington are generally subdivided, the Treasury extension presents the novelty of spacious and airy saloons, capable of accommodating the following bureaus:—

The Secretary's Office, which is charged with the general supervision of the fiscal transactions of the government, and of the execution of the laws concerning the commerce and navigation of the United States. He superintends the survey of the coast, the light-house establishment, the marine hospitals of the United States, and the construction of certain public buildings for custom-houses and other purposes.

The First Comptroller's Office prescribes the mode of keeping and rendering accounts for the civil and diplomatic service, as well as the public lands, and revises and certifies the balances arising thereon.

The Second Comptroller's Office prescribes the mode of keeping and rendering the accounts of the Army, Navy, and Indian Departments of the public service, and revises and certifies the balances arising thereon.

The Office of Commissioner of Customs prescribes the mode of keeping and rendering the accounts of the customs revenue and disbursements, and for the building and repairing custom-houses, &c., and revises and certifies the balances arising thereon.

The First Auditor's Office receives and adjusts the accounts of the customs revenue and disbursements, appropriations and expenditures on account of the civil list and under private acts of Congress, and reports the balances to the Commissioner of the Customs and the First Comptroller, respectively, for their decision thereon.

The Second Auditor's Office receives and adjusts all accounts relating to the pay, clothing, and recruiting of the army, as well as armories, arsenals, and ordnance, and all accounts relating to the Indian bureau, and reports the balances to the Second Comptroller for his decision thereon.

The Third Auditor's Office adjusts all accounts for subsistence of the army, fortifications, military academy, military roads, and the quartermaster's department, as well as for pensions, claims arising from military services previous to 1816, and for horses and other property lost in the military service, under various acts of Congress, and reports the balances to the Second Comptroller for his decision thereon.

The Fourth Auditor's Office adjusts all accounts for the service of the Navy Department, and reports the balances to the Second Comptroller for his decision thereon.

The Fifth Auditor's Office adjusts all accounts for diplomatic and similar services performed under the direction of the State Department, and reports the balances to the First Comptroller for his decision thereon.

The Sixth Auditor's Office adjusts all accounts arising from the service of the Post Office Department. His decisions are final, unless an appeal be taken in twelve months to the First Comptroller. He superintends the collection of all debts due the Post Office Department, and all penalties and forfeitures imposed on postmasters and mail contractors for failing to do their duty; he directs suits and legal proceedings, civil and criminal, and takes all such measures as may be authorized by law to enforce the prompt payment of moneys due to the department,—instructing United States attorneys, marshals, and clerks, on all matters relating thereto,—and receives returns from each term of the United States courts of the condition and progress of such suits and legal proceedings; has charge of all lands and other property assigned to the United States in payment of debts due the Post Office Department, and has power to sell and dispose of the same for the benefit of the United States.

The Treasurer's Office receives and keeps the moneys of the United States in his own office and that of the depositories created by the act of August 6th, 1846, and pays out the same upon warrants drawn by the Secretary of the Treasury, countersigned by the First Comptroller, and upon warrants drawn by the Postmaster-General, and countersigned by the Sixth Auditor, and recorded by the Register. He also holds public moneys advanced by warrant to disbursing officers, and pays out the same upon their checks.

The Register's Office keeps the accounts of public receipts and expenditures; receives the returns, and makes out the official statement of commerce and navigation of the United States; and receives from the First Comptroller and Commissioner of Customs all accounts and vouchers decided by them, and is charged by law with their safe keeping.

The Solicitor's Office superintends all civil suits commenced by the United States (except those arising in the Post Office Department), and instructs the United States' attorneys, marshals, and clerks, in all matters relating to them and their results. He receives returns from each term of the United States courts, showing the progress and condition of such suits; has charge of all lands and other property assigned to the United States in payment of debts (except those assigned in payment of debts due the Post Office Department), and has power to sell and dispose of the same for the benefit of the United States.

The Light-House Board, of which the Secretary of the Treasury is ex-officio president, but in the deliberations of which he has the assistance of naval, military, and scientific coadjutors.

United States Coast Survey. The Superintendent, with numerous assistants employed in the office and upon the survey of the coast, are under the control of this department. A statement of their duties will be found in the next chapter.

Being charged with the collection of the revenue, the semi-naval service known as the Revenue Service is very properly placed in the control of this department, and is not identified with the United States Navy.

Some idea of the magnitude and importance of this executive branch of the government may be formed by an examination of the following statement of the value of foreign merchandise imported, re-exported, and consumed annually, from 1821 to 1859, inclusive, and the estimated population and rate of consumption *per capita* during the same period :—

Years Ending—		Value of Foreign Merchandise.			Popula-tion.	Consump'n per capita.
		Imported	Re-export-ed.	Consumed and on hand.		
September 30,	1821....	$62,585,724	$21,202,488	$41,283,236	9,960,974	$4 14
	1822....	83,241,541	22,286,202	60,955,339	10,283,757	5 92
	1823....	77,579 26.	27,543,622	50,035,645	10,606,540	4 71
	1824....	80,549,007	25,337,157	55,211,850	10,929,328	5 05
	1825....	96,340,075	32,590,643	63,749,432	11,252,106	5 66
	1826....	84,974,477	24,539,612	60,434,865	11,574,889	5 22
	1827....	79,484,068	23,403,136	56,080,932	11,897,672	4 71
	1828....	88,509,824	21,595,017	66,914,807	12,220,455	5 47
	1829....	74,492,527	16,658,478	57,834,049	12,243,238	4 61
	1830....	70,876,920	14,387,479	56,489,441	12,566,020	4 89
	1831....	103,191,124	20,033,526	83,157,598	13,286,864	6 25
	1832....	101,029,266	24,039,473	76,989,793	13,706,707	5 61
	1833....	108,118,311	19,822,735	88,295,576	14,127,050	6 25
	1834....	226,521,832	23,312,811	103,208,521	14,547,398	7 09
	1835....	149,895,742	20,504,495	129,891,247	14,967,736	9 64
	1836....	159,950,035	21,746,860	168,233,675	15,388,079	10 93
	1837....	140,989,217	21,854,962	119,134,255	15,808,422	7 53
	1838....	113,717,404	12,452,795	101,264,609	16,228,765	6 23
	1839....	162,092,132	17,494,525	144,597,607	16,649,108	8 63
	1840....	107,141,519	18,190,312	88,951,207	17,069,453	5 21
	1841....	127,946,177	15,469,081	112,477,096	17,612,507	6 38
	1842....	100,162,057	11,721,548	88,440,549	18,155,561	4 87
9 months to June 30,	1843....	64,753,799	6,552,697.	58,201,102	18,698,615	3 11
Year to June 30,	1844....	108,435,085	11,484,867	96,950,165	19,241,670	5 03
	1845....	117,254,564	15,346,830	101,907,784	19,784,725	5 15
	1846....	121,691,797	11,346,623	110,345,174	20,327,780	5 42
	1847....	146,545,638	8,011,158	138,534,480	20,780,835	6 60
	1848....	154,998,928	21,128,010	133,870,918	21,413,890	6 25
	1849....	147,857,439	13,058,865	134,765,574	21,956,945	6 13
	1850....	178,138,318	14,951,808	163,186,510	23,246,301	7 02
	1851....	216,224,932	21,698,293	194,526,639	24,250,000	8 02
	1852....	212,945,442	17,289,882	195,656,060	24,580,000	8 10
	1853....	267,973,047	17,558,400	250,420,187	25,000,000	10 00
	1854....	304,562,381	24,850,191	279,712,187	25,750,000	10 00
	1855....	261,468,520	28,448,293	233,020,227	26,500,000	8 79
	1856...	314,639,942	16,378,578	298,261,364	27,400,000	10 88
	1857....	360,690,141	23,975,617	336,914,524	28,500,000	11 82
	1858....	282,618,150	80,836,142	251,727,008	29,500,000	8 50
	1859....	838,763,180	20,895,077	317,878,063	30,885,000	10 46

DEPARTMENT OF WAR.

The exigencies to which the colonies were exposed forced them at an early period to concentrate their defensive power. The military successes of Washington and his generals were greatly retarded by the cumbersome arrangements of direct correspondence with and instructions from Congress, in which parties and cliques were frequently stronger than patriotism ; the frozen and bleeding feet of revolutionary soldiers, as at Valley Forge, being sometimes counted of less consequence than the interest of controlling votes. The first recorded legislation of importance upon the military affairs of the nation is the act of Congress of the twenty-seventh day of January, 1785, entitled "An Ordinance for ascertaining the Powers and Duties of the Secretary at War." By this Act the duties of the Secretary are defined ; and amongst them is a provision requiring him to visit " at least once a year," " all the ' magazines and deposits of public stores, and report the state of them, with proper arrangements, to Congress." Immediately after the confederation of the States by the adoption of the Constitution, this legislation was superseded by an act of Congress, approved on the seventh day of August, 1789, defining the duties of the department ; which was again modified by the fifth Congress, in the act of the thirtieth day of April, 1798: "To establish an Executive Department, to be denominated the Department of the Navy." Of the efficiency of this department, and its services to the republic, there can be no better testimony than that which has been extorted from history, in the following words: "The United States, from the peace of Independence, in 1783, achieved by war and merely acknowledged by treaty, have always (?) lost by treaty, but never by war." This sentiment, which is not as true now of our relations with Great Britain as in 1814, contains within it a compliment to the department which, with limited means, and encountering the natural jealousy of civism, has so administered its scanty finances that the army has been made not only a defense for the frontiers, but a recognized national force, able in any emergency to afford a nucleus around which the strength and bravery of the republic may safely crystallize. By the act of the fourteenth of April, 1814, the Secretaries of War and of the Navy were placed in custody of the flags, trophies of war, &c., to deliver the same for presentation and display in such public places as the President may deem proper. Although many trophies which a monarchical power would have jealously preserved have been lost, or at least detached from their proper resting-place, there are still enough in both departments to stir the patriotic emotions of all who take the trouble to inquire for them. The building in which the duties of this important branch of the government are performed is situated on Pennsylvania avenue, west of the Executive Mansion, and will in a few years be replaced by an edifice worthy of description. The present organization of the department is divided amongst the following bureaus :—

Secretary's Office.—The Secretary of War is charged, under the direction of the President, with the general control of the military establishment, and the execution of the laws relating thereto. The functions of the several bureaus are performed under his supervision and authority. In the duties of his immediate office he is assisted by a chief clerk, claims and disbursing clerk, requisition clerk, corresponding clerk, registering clerk, and three recording clerks.

The Adjutant-General's Office is the medium of communication to the army of all general and special orders of the Secretary of War relating to matters of military detail. The rolls of the army and the records of service are kept, and all military commissions prepared, in this office.

The Quartermaster-General's Office has charge of all matters pertaining to barracks and quarters for the troops, transportation, camp and garrison equipage, clothing, fuel, forage, and the incidental expenses of the military establishment.

The Commissary-General's Office has charge of all matters relating to the procurement and issue of subsistence stores to the army.

The Paymaster-General's Office has the general direction of matters relating to the pay of the army.

The Surgeon-General's Office has charge of all matters relating to the medical and hospital service.

The Engineer's Office, at the head of which is the chief engineer of the army, has charge of all matters relating to the construction of the fortifications, and to the military academy. At present the Washington Aqueduct is being built under its direction.

The Bureau of Topographical Engineers, at the head of which is the chief of the corps, has charge of all matters relating to river and harbor improvements, the survey of the lakes, the construction of military roads, and generally of all military surveys.

The Ordnance Bureau, at the head of which is the chief of ordnance, has charge of all matters relating to the manufacture, purchase, storage, and issue of all ordnance, arms, and munitions of war. The management of the arsenals and armories is conducted under its orders.

Exclusive of the office of the Commanding General, there are ninety-five persons, military and clerical, employed in the business of the department.

Between this building and the Navy Department, which is directly to the south of it, there is a large mass of copper from Ontonagon, Lake Superior. This curiosity cost the United States $5,654. It was originally used by the Indians as a sacrificial rock, and they regarded it with a peculiar awe and veneration, in the belief that if seen by a white man, the control of the country would pass out of their hands. The following thrilling description of a human sacrifice once offered on this block of copper, is from the pen of Father Charlevoix, a Jesuit missionary:

In my first voyage to the country, I had heard of the Manitou of the savages, which was of pure copper, and used as a place of sacrifice. * * * * * I listened with horror to the circumstances that attended the sacrifice of a young female, who had been taken prisoner during an excursion of a war-party of the natives.

An expedition had been resolved upon, and they thus thought to insure success and the favor of their powerful Manitou. The young maiden was only fifteen years old. After having a lodge appointed for her use, attendants to meet every wish, her neck, arms, and ankles covered with bracelets of silver and copper, she was led to believe she was to be the bride of the son of the head chief. The time appointed was the end of winter; and she felt rejoiced as the time rolled on, waiting for the season of her happiness.

The day fixed upon for the sacrifice having dawned, she passed through all the preparatory ceremonies, and was dressed in her best attire, covered with all the ornaments the settlement could command; after which she was placed in the midst of a circle of warriors dressed in their war suits, who seemed to escort her for the purpose of showing her deference. Besides their usual arms, each one carried several pieces of wood which he had received from the girl. She had carried wood to the rock on the preceding day which she had helped gather in the forest. Believing she was to be elevated to a high rank, her ideas being of the most pleasing character, the poor girl advanced to the altar with rapturous feelings of joy and timidity, which would naturally be raised in the bosom of a young female of her age. As the procession proceeded, which occupied some time, savage music accompanied them, and chaunts invoking the intervention of their Manitou, that the Great Spirit would prosper their enterprise; so that, being excited by the music and dancing, the deceitful delusion under which she had been kept remained till the last moment. But as soon as they had reached the place of sacrifice, where nothing was to be seen but fires, torches, and instruments of torture, her eyes were opened—her fate was revealed to her—and she became aware of her horrible destiny, as she had often heard of the mysterious sacrifices of the Copper Rock.

She conjured the stern warriors who surrounded her to have pity on her youth, her innocence, but all in vain; the Indian priests coolly proceeded with the horrid ceremonies. * * * She was tied with withes to the top of the rock. The fire was gradually applied to her body with torches made of the wood which she had with her own hands distributed to the warriors. When exhausted with her cries, and about expiring, her tormentors opened the circle that surrounded her, and the great chief shot an arrow into her heart, which was followed by the spears and arrows of his followers, which, after being turned and twisted in the wounds, were torn from her body in such a manner that it presented but one shapeless mass of human flesh, and the blood poured down the glistening sides of the rock in streams. When the blood had ceased to flow, the high priest approached the body of the victim, and, to crown the horrible deed, tore out her heart, and after invoking the blessing of the bloody Manitou, devoured the bleeding flesh, amid the acclamations of the whole tribe. The mangled remains were then left to be destroyed by wild beasts. Their weapons were sprinkled with her blood to render them invincible, and all retired to their cabins cheered and encouraged with the hope of a glorious victory.

NAVY DEPARTMENT.

This department of the government, as we have intimated above, is the child of the War Department. The first intention of the fathers of the American Republic seems to have been simply to provide for a chief clerk under whose direction contracts might be made for munitions of war, and the inspection of provisions necessary for carrying on war by land or sea. As the maritime warfare of the United States increased in the brilliancy of its victories, the necessity for a separate organization to control its officers and to provide for the feeding, equipment, and payment of its seafaring warriors gradually became apparent; but it was not until the thirtieth day of April, 1798, that Congress was sufficiently apprised of this necessity to pass and secure the approval of an act " to establish an Executive Department, to be denominated the Department of the Navy," and on the twenty-second of June of the same year an act was passed granting the franking privilege to the Secretary of the Navy. Subsequent legislation has dealt more with the *morale* of the navy than with the functions of the department; reference to various other

acts is therefore omitted. The building in which the
duties of the department are at present discharged is immediately behind the War Department, and its architecture is so manifestly faulty and meagre that we defer a
description until it shall have a dwelling-place to some
extent commensurate with the important interests it con-
trols and represents. As organized in 1860, the department consists of the following officials :—The Secretary ;
Chief Clerk ; Bureau of Navy Yards and Docks ; Bureau
of Construction, Equipment, and Repairs ; Bureau of Provisions and Clothing ; Bureau of Ordnance and Hydrography ; and the Bureau of Medicine and Surgery ;
comprising in all, including the head of the department,
and exclusive of messengers, forty-nine persons. The
division of labor is as follows :—

Secretary's Office.—The Secretary has charge of everything connected with the naval establishment, and the
execution of all laws relating thereto is intrusted to him,
under the general direction of the President of the United
States, who, by the Constitution, is commander-in-chief
of the army and navy. All instructions to commanders
of squadrons and commanders of vessels, all orders of
officers, commissions of officers both in the navy and
marine corps, appointments of commissioned and warrant
officers, orders for the enlistment and discharge of seamen, emanate from the Secretary's office. All the duties
of the different bureaus are performed under the authority
of the Secretary, and their orders are considered as ema-
nating from him. The general superintendence of the
marine corps forms also a part of the duties of the Secretary, and all the orders of the commandant of that corps
should be approved by him.

Bureau of Navy Yards and Docks.—Chief of the bureau, four clerks, one civil engineer, and one draughtsman. All the navy yards, docks, and wharves, buildings and machinery in navy yards, and everything immediately connected with them, are under the superintendence of this bureau. It is also charged with the management of the Naval Asylum.

Bureau of Construction, Equipment, and Repair.—Chief of the bureau, eight clerks and one draughtsman. The office of the Engineer-in-chief of the Navy, who is assisted by three assistant engineers, is attached to this bureau. This bureau has charge of the building and repairs of all vessels of war, purchase of materials, and the providing of all vessels with their equipments, as sails, anchors, water-tanks, &c. The Engineer-in-chief superintends the construction of all marine steam-engines for the navy, and, with the approval of the Secretary, decides upon plans for their construction.

Bureau of Provisions and Clothing.—Chief of bureau and four clerks. All provisions for the use of the navy, and clothing, together with the making of contracts for furnishing the same, come under the charge of this bureau.

Bureau of Ordnance and Hydrography.—Chief of bureau, four clerks, and one draughtsman. This bureau has charge of all ordnance and ordnance stores, the manufacture or purchase of cannon, guns, powder, shot, shells, &c., and the equipment of vessels of war, with everything connected therewith. It also provides them with maps, charts, chronometers, barometers, &c., together with such books as are furnished to ships of war. "The United States Naval Observatory and Hydrographical Office" at

Washington, and the Naval Academy at Annapolis, are also under the general superintendence of the chief of this bureau.

Bureau of Medicine and Surgery.—Chief of bureau, one passed assistant surgeon United States Navy, and two clerks. Everything relating to medicines and medical stores, treatment of sick and wounded, and management of hospitals, comes within the superintendence of this bureau.

The following statistics may be interesting to some of our readers: In 1806, the number of seamen authorized by law was 925, to which number 3,600 were added in 1809. In 1812, Congress authorized the President to employ as many as would be necessary to equip the vessels to be put in service, and to build as many vessels for the lakes as the public service required. In January, 1814, there were in actual service seven frigates, two corvettes, seven sloops of war, two blockships, four brigs, and three schooners, for sea, besides the several lake squadrons, gunboats, and harbor barges; three ships of the line and three frigates on the stocks. The whole number of men and officers employed was thirteen thousand, three hundred and thirty-nine, of which 3,729 were able seamen, and 6,721 ordinary; the marine corps, as enlarged in 1814, was 2,700 men and officers. The commissioned naval officers combatant were 22 captains, 18 commanders, 107 lieutenants, and 450 midshipmen. In 1814, Secretary Jones reported to the Senate that there were three 74-gun and three 44-gun ships building; six new sloops of war built; twenty barges and one hundred and twenty-five gunboats employed in the Atlantic waters; 33 vessels of all sizes for sea, afloat or building, and 31

on the lakes. Even in 1813, the energy of this department had led the first Napoleon to issue the following instructions to his Minister of Marine :

You will receive a decree by which I order the
building, at Toulon, at Rochefort, and at Cherbourg, of a
frigate of American construction. I am certain that the
English have had built a considerable number of frigates
on that model. They go better, and they adopt them ;
we must not be behindhand. Those which you will have
built at Toulon, at Rochefort, and at Cherbourg, will ma-
nœuvre in the roads, and give us to understand what to
think of the model.

PATENT OFFICE AND DEPARTMENT OF THE
INTERIOR.

We have been compelled to adopt the illogical designation above given for this portion of the chapter, by reason of the fact that the Department of the Interior has no
title to its present quarters in the building belonging to
and mostly paid for by the earnings of the Patent Office.
At first a single room was demanded for the Secretary of

the Interior, and from that the department has continued to annex room after room of the noble building devoted to the protection of the inventive genius of the country, until the bureau for whose especial accommodation the edifice was erected finds itself "cabined and confined" in a corner of the house built with the proceeds of its own industry. The lawful fees charged for issuing patents having largely accumulated, were directed by Congress to be invested, with an additional appropriation, in the Patent Office building. From this commencement, the stately marble palace on the corner of Seventh and F streets has gradually been reared into its present magnificent proportions, the principal architectural credit being due to Mr. Edward Clark. The building is in the Doric style of architecture, 406½ feet by 275, and 74 feet 11 inches in height, divided into three stories of rooms, including the model-room, which occupies the whole upper floor, making in reality four saloons, in beauty unequaled by any apartment in the world, the total length of the connected chambers being upwards of 1,300 feet.

In the court-yard are two fountains, which cool the air in the sultry days of summer. The north front is the only one which has not a portico, and as it would only involve an expense of $75,000 to finish it in the same style with the other fronts, it is to be hoped that Congress will not withhold that sum, especially as the cost of the building would still be within the original estimate.

The Department of the Interior proper, consists of the Secretary, chief clerk, three disbursing clerks, and twelve other regular clerks; and to its supervision and management are committed the following branches of the public service :—

Public Lands.—The chief of this bureau is called the Commissioner of the General Land Office. The land bureau is charged with the survey, management, and sale of the public domain, and the issuing of titles therefor, whether derived from confirmations of grants made by former governments, by sales, donations, grants for schools, military bounties, or public improvements; and likewise the revision of Virginia military bounty-land claims, and the issuing of script in lieu thereof. The land office also audits its own accounts. Its principal officers are a recorder, chief clerk, who also acts as Commissioner *ad interim*, principal clerk of surveys, a draughtsman, assistant draughtsman, and about one hundred and fifty clerks of various grades.

Pensions.—The Commissioner is charged with the examination and adjudication of all claims arising under the various laws passed by Congress granting bounty land or pensions for military or naval services in the revolutionary and subsequent wars in which the United States have been engaged. The Commissioner has one chief clerk, and a permanent corps consisting of seventy other clerks. About a million of dollars are annually disbursed by this bureau.

Indian Affairs.—This office has charge of all matters relating to the Aborigines, and is conducted by a Commissioner, chief clerk, and a clerical force from fifteen to thirty in number. The average annual expenditure on Indian account, including the interest on stocks held in trust for the several tribes, and on sums which, by treaty provision, it was stipulated should be invested, but which have remained in the treasury of the United States, is over $3,000,000 The amount of stock held in trust for Indian tribes by the Department of the Interior is $3,449,241 82, and the net annual interest thereon is $202,002 89.　The present liabilities of the United States to Indian tribes, funding at five per cent. the perpetual annuities secured to some of them by treaty and also the annuities payable during the pleasure of Congress, amount to $21,472,423 88.　This amount is made up of the following items, viz. :

Principal, at five per cent., of permanent annuities, guaranteed by treaty, including amounts which it is stipulated by treaty shall be invested, but which are retained in the Treasury, and on which the United States pay interest,	$7,013,087 80
Temporary annuities guaranteed by treaty, all of which will cease in a limited period	13,295,936 08
Principal, at five per cent., of temporary annuities, payable during the pleasure of the President or of Congress	1,163,400 00
	$21,472,423 88

The Patent Office not only supports itself, but gradually accumulates a fund which will compensate for the construction of its magnificent building, without taxing the people. Its funds are derived from services rendered. It is intrusted with the special duty of granting letters patent, securing a proper compensation to him who discovers or invents that which benefits his fellow-men.　This is not in the nature of a monopoly, as has been sometimes suggested, for the government requires only the estimated cost of investigation and registry.　The bureau of Patents, as the organ of the United States, virtually says to the

ingenuity and intelligence of the world: "If you can
devise a simpler mode of performing any sort of labor,
you shall receive a recompense in proportion to the benefit you confer upon those who ought to pay you." The
table below will show the receipts and expenditures of
this branch of the government from 1837 (the earliest
period at which we have been able to obtain reliable
statistics) to 1860:

Years.	Applica-tions filed	Cavea's filed.	Patents issued.	Cash received.	Cash expended.
1837....	....	....	435	$29,289 08	$33,506 98
1838....	....	....	520	42,123 54	37,402 10
1839....	....	....	425	37,260 00	34,543 51
1840...	....	....	473	38,056 51	39,020 67
1841....	....	....	495	40,413 01	52,666 87
1842....	761	291	517	36,505 68	31,241 43
1843....	819	315	531	35,315 81	30,776 96
1844....	1,045	380	502	42,509 26	36,344 73
1845....	1,246	452	502	51,076 14	39,395 65
1846....	1,272	448	619	50,264 16	46,158 71
1847....	1,531	533	572	63,111 19	41,878 35
1848....	1,628	607	660	67,576 69	58,905 84
1849....	1,955	595	1,070	80,752 78	77,716 44
1850....	2,193	602	995	86,927 05	80,100 95
1851....	2,258	700	869	95,738 61	86,916 93
1852....	2,639	996	1,020	112,056 34	95,916 91
1853....	2,673	901	958	121,527 45	132,869 83
1854....	3,324	868	1,902	163,789 84	167,146 32
1855....	4,435	906	2,024	216 459 35	179,540 33
1856....	4,960	1,024	2,502	192,588 02	199,931 02
1857....	4,771	1,010	2,910	196,132 01	211,582 09
1858....	5,364	943	3,710	203,716 16	193,193 74
1859....	6,225	1,097	4,538	265,942 15	210,278 41
1860....	....	....	4,819	256,352 59	252,820 80

The whole number of patents issued by the office,
from July, 1836, to Dec. 31st, 1860, was 31,004, than
which fact we know of no more startling commentary
upon the extraordinary development of the mechanical

and mathematical powers of the American mind during the last quarter of a century. In Great Britain the issue of patents for inventions from March 2d, 1617 (the date of the first Letters of Patent), to December 31st, 1860, has been as follows :—

1617, March 2, to Oct. 1, 1852.........	14,359
Oct. 1, to Dec. 31, 1852.............	1,211
1853	3,045
1854	2,764
1855	2,958
1856	3,106
1857	3,200
1858	3,007
1859	3,000
1860 ....over	3,000

To this bureau is committed the execution and performance of all acts and things touching and respecting the granting and issuing of patents for new and useful discoveries, inventions and improvements; the collection of statistics relating to agriculture; the collection and distribution of seeds, plants, and cuttings. It has a chief clerk—who is by law the acting Commissioner of Patents in the absence of the Commissioner—twelve principal, twelve assistant, and several second-assistant examiners of patents.

All books, maps, charts, and other publications heretofore deposited in the Department of State, according to the laws regulating copyrights, go to the Department of the Interior, which is charged with all the duties connected with matters pertaining to copyright, which duties have been assigned by the Secretary of the Interior to the Patent Office, as belonging most appropriately to this branch of the service.

The great national importance of its business requires that the Patent Office should cease to be a mere bureau of the Department of the Interior. In the language of the Hon. J. Thompson, when Secretary: " The increase of business in the Patent Office, and the magnitude of its operations, give additional force to the recommendations heretofore made for a re-organization of this bureau. The amount of work devolved upon the examiners is enormous, and it is difficult to believe that the reiterated appeals in their behalf would have been so entirely disregarded, had Congress realized the actual condition of the business of the office ; and as the office is self-sustaining, it is only reasonable that this department should be empowered to graduate the force employed, by the work to be done, provided, always, that the expenditures shall be kept within the receipts."

The income of the office, for the three quarters ending September 30, 1860, was $197,648 40, and its expenditure, $189,672 23, showing a surplus of $7,976 17.

During this period, five thousand six hundred and thirty-eight applications for patents were received, and eight hundred and forty-one caveats filed. Three thousand six hundred and twelve applications were rejected, and three thousand eight hundred and ninety-six patents issued, including re-issues, additional improvements, and designs. In addition to this, there were forty-nine applications for extensions, and twenty-eight patents extended for a period of seven years from the expiration of their first term.

It may not be out of place to suggest to persons hav-

6

ing business to transact with the Patent Office, that the most certain, speedy and economical method they can pursue is to secure the services of a competent attorney, whose fee will be regulated by his professional standing ; in some cases, gentlemen distinguished by a peculiar aptitude for the knotty questions which involve both legal and scientific training, receive very large sums for their services, but it must be borne in mind that it requires a long, patient, and peculiar discipline to prepare one either for an attorney or examiner of patents, of the latter of whom Judge Huntington is reported to have said that the duties were the most arduous of any performed by a public servant, and that a person qualified to discharge them was fitted to be a judge of the supreme court.

The library of the Patent Office contains a collection of volumes of the highest scientific value; under judicious arrangement, a collection already rich and ample is forming, of every work of interest to the inventors, and that new, increasing, important class of professional men, —the attorneys in patent cases. Upon its shelves may be found a complete set of the reports of the British Patent Commissioners, of which there are only six copies in the United States. The reports of French patents are also complete, and those of various other countries are being obtained as rapidly as possible. A system of exchanges has been established, which employs three agents abroad ; and, in addition to various and arduous duties, the librarian annually despatches several hundred copies of the reports.

Besides these four principal branches of this executive department, the organic act of 1849 transferred to it from the Treasury department the supervision of the accounts of the United States marshals, and attorneys, and the clerks of the United States courts, the management of the lead and other mines of the United States, and the affairs of the Penitentiary of the United States in the District of Columbia; and from the State department the duty of taking and returning the censuses of the United States, and of supervising and directing the acts of the Commissioner of Public Buildings. The Hospital for the Insane of the army and navy, and of the District of Columbia, is also under the management of this department; in addition to which the Secretary of the Interior is charged with the construction of the three wagon roads leading to the Pacific coast.

Under the act of February 5, 1858, "providing for keeping and distributing all public documents," all the books, documents, &c., printed or purchased by the government, the Annals of Congress, American State Papers, American Archives, Jefferson's and Adams' Works, are transferred to this department from the State department, library of Congress, and elsewhere; also the journal and documents of the thirty-fifth Congress. These valuable works are distributed to those who are by law entitled to receive them, and to such "colleges, public libraries, atheneums, literary and scientific institutions, boards of trade, or public associations," as shall be designated by the members of Congress.

Census Bureau.—This important bureau is by law placed under control of the Interior department, and will probably become a permanent branch under the designation of Bureau of Statistics. At present it is temporary in its organization, its force being disbanded when the work of each decade is concluded. The following table,

showing the expense incurred in taking the census at different periods, will give some idea of the magnitude of
the duties confided to this unobtrusive bureau :—

DATE	COST OF CENSUS.	POPULATION.
1790	$44,337 28	3,929,827
1800	66,109 04	5,305,925
1810	178,444 67	7,239,814
1820	208,525 99	9,638,131
1830	378,545 13	12,866,020
1840	833,370 95	17,069,453
1850	1,318,027 53	23,191,876
1860	1,642,000 00	

The Agricultural Bureau, established for the purpose
of diffusing information and distributing new varieties of
plants and seeds, is much hampered in its operations by
its relations with the department. Really needing to become a branch of the government distinct from all others
and entirely beyond the fluctuations of political affairs, it
is now confined within the limits the Secretary of the
Interior may choose to indicate. Capable of becoming of
immense national benefit, and already attracting the attention of other nations, it is a pity its operations and organization should be so restricted.

The National Conservatories, under the direction of
this bureau, are situated on the west side of Pennsylvania
avenue, immediately west of the Capitol, where the
soil, unfortunately, is not the most advantageous, being
cold and wet. A recent agricultural report of the Patent
Office, containing a vast amount of very valuable information concerning the garden and green-houses, with their
contents, states that a system of underground tile-drain-

age has been adopted, but, owing to the marshy character of the soil, only partial success has been attained. Referring to the green-houses, it is authoritatively reported that the plan pursued in constructing and warming the green-houses, though successful in its present application, is not commended for all purposes. Decomposing vegetable matter, covered with a portion of nitrogenous materials, might be adapted to general use, were the process of decomposition susceptible of being controlled at will; but so variable is its progress, and so dependent upon external influences, in a ratio inverse to the requirements within, that the vicissitudes of temperature proceeding from it are such as none but hardy plants can endure. The volatile emanations are likewise in excess in this process, insomuch that even those plants which become accustomed to and prove capable of sustaining an atmosphere so highly stimulating may suffer when suddenly withdrawn from its influence and exposed to the open air. The partial exclusion of light and warmth of the sun, practiced in connection with this plan, also proves detrimental to tender plants.

A catalogue of the plants, prepared by Mr. W. R. Smith, an accomplished botanist, may be found in the Guide to the Curiosities of the Patent Office. We will only add a few remarks about the tea-plant, of which there were procured 32,000 plants for distribution, of which, so rare was it in 1664, that the Dutch East India Company presented two pounds and two ounces of it to Charles II., King of England, which country consumes annually about thirty millions of pounds, while the people of the United States submit to a voluntary tea tax of about eight millions of dollars. The tea-plant is an evergreen, bearing a re-

semblance to the camelia, and in a wild state growing to
the height of ten feet, and, when cultivated, dwarfed to
three or four, by pinching off the leading shoots, to force
it to throw out numerous little shoots from which to
obtain leaves. The crop upon an acre of ground generally averages as follows :—3d year, 10 pounds; 4th year, .
30 pounds; 5th year, 80 pounds; 6th year, 120 pounds;
7th year, 150 pounds; 8th year, 200 pounds; 9th year,
250 pounds; 10th year, 300 pounds. For further interesting information respecting this and other valuable
plants the reader is referred to the Patent Office Report on
Agriculture for 1859. The public is greatly indebted to
the Hon. J. A. Pearce, who has been the congressional
fosterer of this useful and beautiful garden, and also to
Capt. Wilkes and other gallant naval officers who have
contributed to its riches.

POST OFFICE DEPARTMENT.

The progress of a country is so vitally dependent
upon its postal facilities, and so well illustrated by the description of the mail facilities afforded to the people at
various periods of its history that we regret the limits
allowed by the necessity of a hurried appearance before
the public prevent our furnishing an essay upon the history of the Post Office Department. As it is, we are
compelled to say, in brief, that as early as the year 1692
the English colonies in America were so impressed with
the importance of postal facilities that the colony of Virginia attempted to introduce a system of mail arrangements; a proposition was at that date introduced into
the Assembly of Virginia to confer upon Mr. Neal the

responsibilities of Postmaster-General of Virginia *and other parts of America.* The Assembly indorsed this proposition by passing act establishing the office, but owing to the inchoate condition of public affairs it was never carried into effect. In 1710, by an act of the British Parliament, a General Post Office for all Her Majesty's* dominions was established, and the Postmaster-General was permitted to have "one chief letter-office in New York, and other chief letter offices at some convenient place or places in each of Her Majesty's provinces or colonies in America." When the colonies resolved to demand their rights, they were careful at an early day to preserve the opportunities for epistolary communications between the citizens of the colonies. An act was early passed by the deputies from the colonies to secure this end. The Continental Congress provided with jealous care for the accomplishment of the same object, and with the confederation of the States, the Constitution adopted 17th September, 1787, reserved to Congress the right "to establish post offices and post roads." In 1789, Congress enacted a law providing for the appointment of a Postmaster-General and defining his duties. Other laws have been enacted since, from time to time, but the magnitude of the interests confided to this department is such that the Postmaster-General has become a Cabinet officer, and is not only required to regulate the vast concerns of his department, but in addition to assist in the deliberations which decide the home and foreign policy of the Government.

The Post Office building occupies the block situated on Seventh and Eighth streets west, and E and F streets

* Queen Anne, of England.

north. In the centre of the edifice there is a court yard occupying the space of 95 feet by 194. The architecture is a modified Corinthian, and is the best representation of the Italian palatial ever erected upon this continent, re-

POST OFFICE BUILDING.

flecting the highest credit upon its designers, of whom we are compelled to say that T. U. Walter is, in our simple judgment, entitled to the highest meed of praise. By the recent enlargement, this building has been so extended as to develop the elegant proportions of its architectural lines, and were it in any other position but under the great shadow of the magnificent Patent Office, it would be deemed a marvel of architectural beauty. On the Seventh-street side there is a vestibule, the ceiling of which is composed of richly ornamented marbles, supported by four marble columns; the walls, niches, and floors, are also of marble, finely polished, the floor being richly tesselated. This is the grand entrance for the General Post Office department. The entrance for the mail wagons on Eighth street consists of a grand archway, the spandrils of which are ornamented with sculpture representing Steam and

Electricity, while a mask representing Fidelity forms the key-stone. The F street front is arranged for the accommodation of the city Post Office ; it has a deeply-recessed portico in the centre, consisting of eight columns grouped in pairs, and flanked by coupled pilasters, supporting an entablature which girds the entire work. The portico is supported by an arcade, which furnishes the most ample convenience for the delivery of letters to the public. The columns of this portico are each of them formed of a single block of marble, and are very beautiful both in design and execution.

The Postmaster-General has assigned to him the direction and management of all postal affairs. That the business may be the more conveniently arranged and prepared for his final action, it is distributed among several bureaus, as follows : the Appointment Office, in charge of the First Assistant Postmaster-General ; the Contract Office, in charge of the Second Assistant Postmaster-General ; the Finance Office, in charge of the Third Assistant Postmaster-General ; and the Inspection Office, in charge of the Chief Clerk

Appointment Office.—First Assistant Postmaster-General, and nineteen clerks. To this office is assigned all questions which relate to the establishment and discontinuance of post-offices, changes of sites and names, appointment and removal of postmasters, route and local agents ; as, also, the giving of instructions to postmasters ; postmasters are furnished with marking and rating stamps, and letter-balances by this bureau, which is charged also with providing blanks and stationery for the use of the department, and with the superintendence of

6*

the several agencies established for supplying postmasters
with blanks. To this bureau is likewise assigned the supervision of the ocean mail steamship lines, and of the
foreign and international postal arrangement.

Contract Office.—Second Assistant Postmaster-General, and twenty-six clerks. To this office is assigned the
business of arranging the mail service of the United
States, and placing the same under contract, embracing
all correspondence and proceedings respecting the fre-
quency of trips, mode of conveyance, and times of departures and arrivals on all the routes ; the course of the
mails between the different sections of the country, the
points of mail distribution, and the regulations of the
government of the domestic mail service of the United
States. It prepares the advertisements for mail propo-
sals, receives the bids, and takes charge of the annual and
occasional mail-letting, and the adjustment and execution
of the contracts. All applications for the establishment
or alteration of mail-messengers, should be sent to this
office. All claims for transportation service not under
contract should be submitted to it, as the recognition of
said service is first to be obtained through the Contract
Office as a necessary authority for the proper credits at the
Auditor's Office. From this office all postmasters at the
ends of routes receive the statement of the mail
arrangements prescribed for their respective routes. It
reports weekly to the Auditor all contracts executed, and
all orders affecting accounts for mail transportation ; prepares the statistical exhibits of the mail service, and the
reports of the mail-lettings, giving statement of each
bid ; also, the contracts made, the new service originated,

the curtailments ordered, and the additional allowances granted within the year.

Finance Office.—Third Assistant Postmaster-General, and twenty-one clerks. This office has the supervision and management of the financial business of the department, not devolved by law upon the Auditor, embracing accounts with the draft-offices and other depositories of the department, the issuing of warrants and drafts in payment of balances reported by the Auditor to be due to mail contractors and other persons, the supervision of the accounts of offices under orders to deposit their quarterly balances at designated points, and the superintendence of the rendition by postmasters of their quarterly returns of postages. It has charge of the dead-letter office, of the issuing of postage-stamps and stamped envelopes for the prepayment of postage, and of the accounts connected therewith.

To the Third Assistant Postmaster-General all postmasters should direct their quarterly returns of postage; those at draft-offices, their letters reporting quarterly the net proceeds of their offices; and those at depositing offices their certificates of deposit; to him should also be directed the weekly and monthly returns of the depositories of the department, as well as all applications and receipts for postage-stamps and stamped envelopes, and for dead letters.

Inspection Office.—Chief clerk, and seventeen clerks. To this office is assigned the duty of receiving and examining the registers of the arrival and departures of the mails, certificates of the service of route agents, and reports of mail failures; noting the delinquencies of contractors, and preparing cases thereon for the action of the Postmaster-General; furnishing blanks for mail registers and reports of mail failures; providing and sending out mail bags and mail locks and keys, and doing all other things which may be necessary to secure a faithful and exact performance of all mail contracts.

All cases of mail depredation, of violations of law by private expresses, or by the forging and illegal use of postage stamps, are under the supervision of this office, and should be reported to it.

All communications respecting lost money-letters, mail depredations, or other violations of law, or mail locks and keys, should be directed " Chief Clerk, Post Office Department."

All registers of the arrivals and departures of the mails, certificates of the service of route agents, reports of mail failures, applications for blank registers, and all complaints against contractors for irregular or imperfect service, should be directed " Inspection Office, Post Office Department."

CHAPTER IV.

THE LEGISLATIVE DEPARTMENT.

THE CAPITOL.

THIS magnificent edifice is situated upon the brow of the eastern plateau of the city, ninety feet above the low-tide level of the Potomac. Its commanding position was determined by Washington, as an imposing site, overlooking the city like the Acropolis at Athens.

The building fronts the east, having been set by an astronomical observation by Andrew Ellicott; and is surrounded by a beautiful park of thirty-five acres, adorned with a great variety of shade-trees, both indigenous and foreign. The Capitol stands in latitude 38° 55′ 48″ north, and longitude 77° 1′ 48″ west from Greenwich. The calculation was made in 1821, by William Lambert, from observations by William Elliot, by authority of Congress.

The design of the central portion, including the old wings, was presented by Dr. William Thornton, and accepted by President Washington, according to act of Congress. The architecture is of the Corinthian order, though not limited to any particular  example, while some of the capitals of columns are original in design. The general features of the exterior of the entire building are in conformity, although the types of the order are quite varied in the interior, and the Doric order is employed in some instances in the basement.

The corner-stone was laid, at the southeast corner of the north wing, by Washington, at twelve o'clock meridian, on Wednesday, September 18, 1793, with all the Masonic rites appropriate to the occasion. A grand Masonic, military, and civic procession was formed on the square in front of the President's mansion, from whence it proceeded to the Capitol ground, with martial music and flying colors, attended by an immense concourse of rejoicing spectators. Arrived at the foundation of the Capitol, the Grand Sword Bearer, followed by the President, marshaled the representatives of the Masonic fraternity between the double lines of the procession, to the corner-stone. After a solemn pause, and the discharge of

artillery, the Grand Marshal delivered to the Commissioners of the District a large silver plate, bearing the following inscription, which was then read :—

This southeast corner stone of the Capitol of the
United States of America, in the city of Washington, was
laid on the 18th day of September, 1793, in the thirteenth
year of American Independence, in the first year of the
second term of the Presidency of George Washington,
whose virtues in the civil administration of his country
have been so conspicuous and beneficial, as his military
valor and prudence have been useful in establishing her
liberties, and in the year of Masonry, 5793, by the President of the United States, in concert with the Grand Lodge
of Maryland, several lodges under its jurisdiction, and
Lodge No. 22 from Alexandria, Virginia.   •

Thomas Johnson, David Stuart, and Daniel Carroll,
Commissioners; Joseph Clarke, R. W. G. M. P. T.;
James Hoban and Stephen Hallet, Architects; Collin
Williamson, M. Mason.

The artillery discharged another volley, when the plate
was delivered to the President, who, attended by the
Grand Master *pro tem.* and three Worshipful Masters, deposited the plate on the corner-stone, upon which was
placed corn, wine, and oil. The assembly joined in prayer,
which was succeeded by the Masonic honors, and a volley
from the artillery. An oration was then delivered by the
Grand Master *pro tem.*, and the ceremony was concluded
by a prayer, Masonic honors, and fifteen rounds from the
artillery. The assemblage retired to an extensive booth,
where they enjoyed a barbecue feast, and the celebration
was concluded with another salute of fifteen guns at sun-
set.

Under the successive superintendence of Stephen Hallet, George Hadfield, and James Hoban, as architects, the

north wing was made available for the first sitting of Congress in Washington, Nov. 17, 1800. In the meantime the walls of the south wing were carried up twenty feet and roofed over, for the temporary occupation of the House of Representatives. The House sat in this building, which was styled " the oven," from 1802 until 1804, when the roof was removed for the completion of the wing, under the direction of B. H. Latrobe, while the House occupied the room of the Library of Congress, on the west side of the north wing, until the hall in the south wing was prepared for use, in 1808.

The old Senate chamber was of but temporary construction, the columns and entablature being of wood stuccoed, and the capitals of plaster. The staircases were also of wood. On September 19, 1808, the centre of the vault of the old room of the Supreme Court was removed, when the arch gave way, carrying with it the floor of the Senate chamber, and killing John Lenthall, clerk of the works. It was the opinion of Mr. Latrobe that this accident was occasioned by striking the centre of the arch too early. The damage to the building was immediately repaired.

The south wing was finished in 1811, the work having been much delayed by the embargo troubles of 1808 and 1809. The finish of this wing was much more beautiful and substantial than that of the Senate chamber. The Hall of Representatives was semicircular, with a vaulted wooden ceiling ; the entablature was supported by twenty fluted Corinthian columns of sandstone ; the frieze over the Speaker's chair was ornamented by a figure of the American eagle, carved in sandstone, by Signor Franzoni ; the opposite frieze was also decorated with figures by the same artist, representing Agriculture, Commerce, Art, and Science. Behind the chair of the Speaker sat a figure of Liberty, with the eagle by her side, her right hand presenting the Constitution on a scroll, and the liberty-cap in her left, her feet resting upon a reversed crown and other symbols of monarchy and bondage.

The sandstone of which the walls of the central portion of the Capitol are constructed, was procured from an island in Acquia Creek, in Virginia. The island was purchased by the Government, in 1791, for $6,000, for the use of the quarry. The two halls of Congress were connected by a temporary wooden structure, for convenience of communication between the two legislative bodies.

The interior of both wings was destroyed by fire when the British took the city, August 24, 1814, but the outer walls remained uninjured. Latrobe, who had resigned in 1813, was reappointed, immediately after the fire, to reconstruct the building.

Congress sat, during the first session after the invasion, in the Post Office building, and ordered the Capitol to be rebuilt, by act of February 13, 1815; and on the 8th of the following December, passed an act leasing a building situated on the eastern side of the Capitol park, and now known as the Old Capitol. Congress remained in that building until the Capitol was prepared for occupation.

On the resignation of Latrobe, in December, 1817, he was succeeded by Charles Bulfinch, under whose superintendence the foundation of the main building was laid, March 24, 1818, and the original design was finally completed in 1825.

The Capitol Extension.—By the act of Congress, Sep-

tember 30, 1850, provision was made for the extension of
the Capitol, according to such plan as might be approved
by the President. The plan of Thomas U. Walter, architect, was accepted by President Fillmore, June 10, 1851,
and he was appointed to carry it out.

The corner-stone of the extension was laid with imposing ceremonies, which are best described by quoting the
record deposited beneath the stone, which is as follows:—

On the morning of the first day of the seventy-sixth
year of the Independence of the United States of America, in the city of Washington, being the 4th day of July,
1851, this stone, designed as the corner-stone of the extension of the Capitol, according to a plan approved by the
President, in pursuance of an act of Congress, was laid
by

MILLARD FILLMORE,

PRESIDENT OF THE UNITED STATES,

assisted by the Grand Master of the Masonic Lodges, in
the presence of many members of Congress, of officers of
the Executive and Judiciary Departments, National, State,
and District, of officers of the Army and Navy, the Corporate authorities of this and neighboring cities, many
associations, civil and military and masonic, officers of the
Smithsonian Institution and National Institute, professors
of colleges and teachers of schools of the District, with
their students and pupils, and a vast concourse of people
from places near and remote, including a few surviving
gentlemen who witnessed the laying of the corner-stone
of the Capitol by President Washington, on the eighteenth
day of September, seventeen hundred and ninety-three.

If, therefore, it shall be hereafter the will of God that
this structure shall fall from its base, that its foundation
be upturned, and this deposit brought to the eyes of men,
be it then known, that, on this day, the Union of the United
States of America stands firm; that their Constitution still
exists unimpaired, and with all its original usefulness and

glory, growing every day stronger and stronger in the affections of the great body of the American people, and attracting more and more the admiration of the world. And all here assembled, whether belonging to public life or to private life, with hearts devoutly thankful to Almighty God for the preservation of the liberty and happiness of the country, unite in sincere and fervent prayers that this deposit, and the walls and arches, the domes and towers, the columns and entablatures now to be erected over it, may endure forever !

GOD SAVE THE UNITED STATES OF AMERICA.

DANIEL WEBSTER,
Secretary of State of the United States.

Daniel Webster officiated as the orator of the day, and concluded the ceremony by a most eloquent address.

The extension consists of two wings placed at the north and south ends of the former building, at a distance of 44 feet from it, with connecting corridors 56 feet 8 inches wide inclusive of their outside colonnades. Each wing is 142 feet 8 inches in front, on the east, by 238 feet 10 inches in depth, exclusive of the porticoes and steps. The porticoes fronting the east have each twenty-two monolithic fluted columns, and extend the entire width of the front, having central projections of ten feet four inches, forming double porticoes in the centre, the width of the gable. There is also a portico of ten columns on the west end of each wing, 105 feet 8 inches wide, projecting 10 feet 6 inches, and like porticoes on the north side of the north wing and south side of the south wing, with a width of 121 feet 4 inches. The centre building is 352 feet 4 inches long and 121 feet 6 inches deep, with a portico 160 feet wide, of twenty-four columns, with a double façade on the east, and a projection of 83 feet on the west, em-

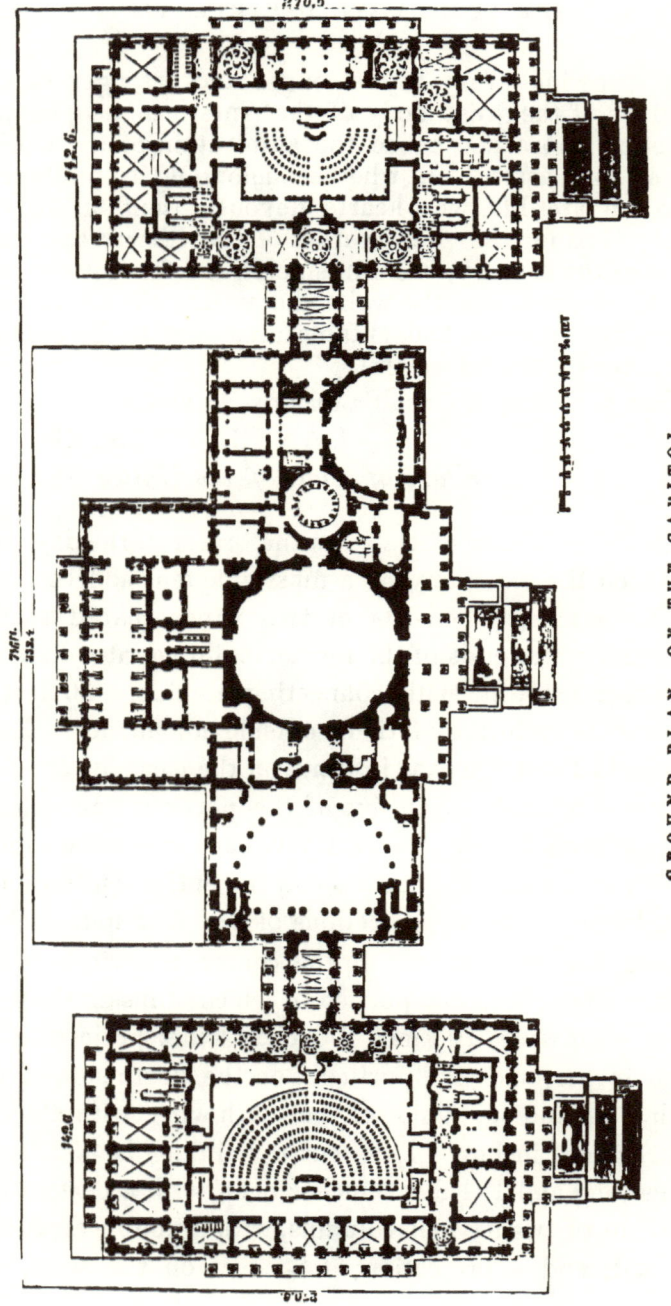

GROUND PLAN OF THE CAPITOL.

bracing a recessed portico of ten coupled columns. The entire length of the Capitol is 751 feet 4 inches, and the greatest depth, including porticoes and steps, is 324 feet. The ground actually covered by the building, exclusive of the court-yards, is 153,112 square feet, or 652 feet over three and a half acres.

The material of which the extension is built, is a white marble slightly variegated with blue, and was procured from a quarry in Lee, Massachusetts. The columns are all of white marble obtained from Maryland.

The principal story of the Capitol rests upon a rustic basement, which supports an ordonnance of pilasters rising to the height of the two stories above. Upon these pilasters rests the entablature and beautiful frieze, and the whole is surmounted by a marble balustrade.

The main entrances are by the three eastern porticoes, being made easy of access by broad flights of stone steps with massive check-blocks, and vaulted carriage-ways beneath to the basement entrances.

The Dome.—Over the rotunda, in the centre of this huge pile, rises a magnificent cast-iron dome. The old dome was constructed of brick, stone, and wood, and sheathed with copper. Its height, inclusive of a circular wooden balustrade upon the top, was 145 feet from the ground. This was removed in 1856, and the present stupendous structure of iron is now taking its place. It was designed by T. U. Walter, the accomplished architect of the extension, and the castings made and erected in their places, by Janes, Beebe & Co., of New York city, who have accomplished in this work the noblest specimen of iron construction of which the world can boast, embody-

APEX OF THE DOME.

ing all the most beautiful forms and proportions of classic
architecture. The exterior presents a noble peristyle,
124 feet in diameter, of fluted columns 27 feet in height,
resting upon an octagonal base or stylobate, which itself is 93 feet above the basement floor. The top of

the entablature of the peristyle is at the height of 127 feet above the basement floor. From this entablature springs an attic 44 feet in height and 108 feet in diameter; and from the cornice of the attic, the great dome, of a semi-ellipsoidal form, rises to a height of 228 feet. The lantern on the top of this dome is 17 feet in diameter, and 52 feet high, and will be crowned by a bronze statue of Liberty, by Crawford, 16 feet 6 inches in height, rising to the height of 300 feet above the basement floor of the building.

Architectural Sculpture.—The tympanum of the central pediment of the capitol is decorated with a group sculptured in alto-relievo, representing the Genius of America, crowned with a star, her right hand holding a shield, inscribed with the letters U. S. A., surrounded with a glory. The shield rests on an altar, bearing the memorable date, " July 4, 1776," within a wreath. Behind her stands a spear, and at her feet, the eagle. Her face is turned towards a figure of Hope, upon the left, whose attention she is directing, by her right hand, to a figure of Justice upon her right, holding the " Constitution of the United States" upon a scroll, in her right hand, and the scales in her left. This group was executed by Signor Persico, and is said to have been designed by John Quincy Adams.

The northern pediment contains a group of sculpture by Thomas Crawford, representing the progress of civilization in the United States. In the centre of the tympanum stands a figure of America in the blaze of a rising sun. On her right are figures of the soldier, commerce, youth and education, the mechanic, and a sheaf of wheat, typical of agriculture. On her left are the pioneer back-

NORTH-EAST PEDIMENT OF THE CAPITOL.

woodsman, the hunter, the Indian and his squaw with an infant in her arms, sitting by a filled grave.

The southern pediment has not yet been filled, although it is understood that a design of the discovery by Columbus has been made for the purpose, by William R. Barbee, the Virginian sculptor. The subject is most appropriate, and no other can properly be substituted for it, since the adoption of the design by Crawford, in completing these most prominent decorations of the architecture. It is essential to commemorate the discovery of the country before we illustrate its progress.

Upon the cheek-blocks of the steps to the central portico, are two groups of statuary. On the north side, the early struggles of our pioneer settlers are symbolized in a group, by Horatio Greenough, representing a sturdy backwoodsman pinioning the arms of an Indian, who is about to dispatch, with his tomahawk, the wife and infant of the white man. A faithful dog stands ready to assist his master in time of need. This spirited work was erected in 1853. In the corresponding position opposite, the discovery of America is typified by Signor Persico, in a statue of Columbus presenting a globe in his hand, while an Indian maiden crouches by his side, gazing at him with mingled wonder and astonishment.

Two of the finest pieces of sculpture about the Capitol are the statues of Mars and Ceres, by Persico, symbolizing War and Peace. They stand in niches on the right and left of the entrance to the rotunda. Immediately over the door, is a fine bas-relief by Signor Capellano, representing Fame and Peace crowning a bust of Washington with wreaths of laurel.

The Rotunda.—This circular room, occupying the centre of the building, is ninety-six feet in diameter, and the entire height of the interior of the dome. It is surrounded by an ordonnance of fluted pilasters thirty feet in height, supporting an entablature and cornice of fourteen feet. Above this cornice a vertical wall will be raised, with a deep recessed panel nine feet in height, to be filled with sculpture, forming a continuous frieze three hundred feet in length, of figures in alto-relievo. The subject to be the History of America. The gradual progress of a continent from the depths of barbarism to the height of civilization; the rude and primitive civilization of some of the ante-Columbian tribes; the contests of the Aztecs with their less civilized predecessors; their own conquest by the Spanish race; the wilder state of the hunter tribes of our own regions; the discovery, settlement, and wars of America; the advance of the white and retreat of the red races; our own revolutionary and other struggles, with an illustration of the higher achievements of our present civilization, will afford a richness and variety of costume, character, and incident, which may worthily employ our best sculptors in its execution, and which will form for future ages a monument of the present state of the arts in this country.

Above the frieze the interior will be enriched by a
7

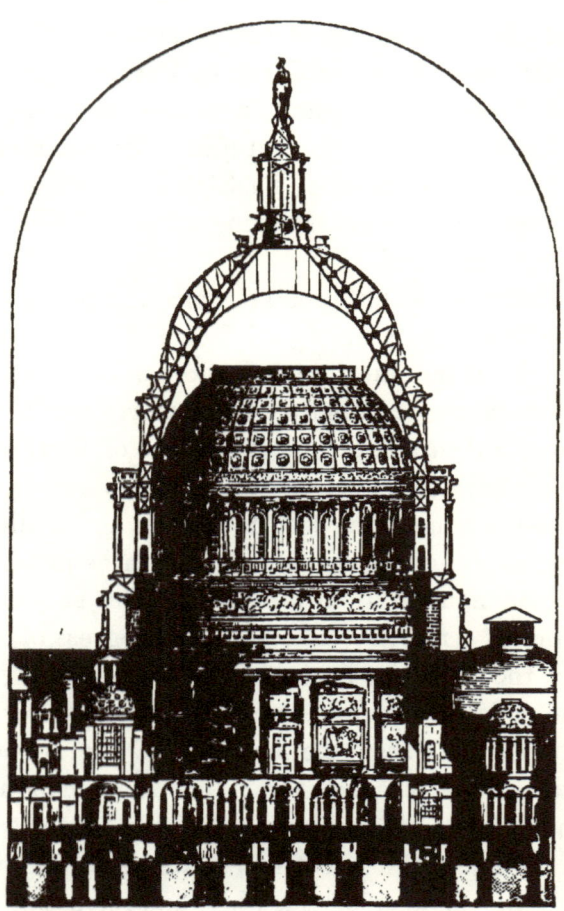

SECTIONAL VIEW OF DOME.

series of attached columns, with large windows in the interspaces, giving ample light to the rotunda.

Above this colonnade a dome will spring, which, contracting to a space of sixty-five feet in diameter, will, through its opening, permit the eye to see another and lighter colonnade at a higher level; the whole being closed in at the base of the lantern, and at a height of 203 feet above the pavement of the rotunda, by a second dome of 73 feet span.

This upper dome, lighted by openings around its base, should be richly painted. Galleries at various heights, approached by stairs between the inner and outer shells of the building, will afford easy access to all parts of the dome, and from thence will be obtained a series of most picturesque views of the interior of the rotunda, and of the beautiful surrounding scenery.

The walls of the rotunda, between the pilasters below, are decorated with eight paintings on canvas, each eighteen feet in length by twelve in height. Four of them are by the hand of Colonel John Trumbull, and illustrate the Declaration of Independence, the Surrender of Burgoyne at Saratoga, the Surrender of Lord Cornwallis at Yorktown, and the Resignation of Washington, as Commander-in-chief of the Army, in 1783. These paintings were ordered by the government, at an expense of $8,000 each, and are valuable and interesting for the portraits they contain. The remaining four are, the Embarcation of the Pilgrims in the Speedwell, at Delft Haven, by Robert W. Weir; the Landing of Columbus, by John Vanderlyn; De Soto's Discovery of the Mississippi, by William H. Powell; and the Baptism of Pocahontas, by John Gadsby Chapman. These were also ordered by Congress, and cost the government from $10,000 to $20,000 each. All these paintings have their faults, either in respect of design, perspective, or color; and yet they all have their individual merits, and are worthy of the study of the artist and connoisseur. The wall above these paintings is ornamented with panels of arabesque in bas-relief.   Four alternate panels contain heads of Columbus, Sir Walter Raleigh, Cabot, and La Salle.

In panels over the four doors of the rotunda, are alto-relievos in stone; Penn's Treaty with the Indians, by M. Gevelot; the Landing of the Pilgrims at Plymouth, by Causici; the Conflict of Daniel Boone with the Indians, by the same artist; and the Rescue of Captain John Smith by Pocahontas, by Capellano.

The floor of the rotunda is of freestone, and is supported by arches of brick, resting upon two concentric peristyles of forty Doric columns in the crypt below. It was the intention of Congress to place the remains of Washington in a mausoleum in the sub-basement, beneath the rotunda, to be made accessible by a spiral staircase descending from the floor.   This project was abandoned in 1832, upon the passage of a resolution by the Virginia legislature, requesting the proprietors of Mount Vernon not to consent to the removal of the remains, and the declension of John A. Washington, on the ground of respect for Washington's Will, directing the disposition of his ashes and those of his family.

The Senate Chamber.—In the centre of the north wing is the chamber of the Senate. Its entrance from the interior of the building is at the termination of a long corridor, extending through the rotunda, and connecting with the door of the Hall of Representatives in the south wing. The main entrance from the exterior is by the eastern portico, through a spacious vestibule, with a marble paneled ceiling, supported by sixteen coupled fluted columns, with capitals beautifully foliated with acanthus and tobacco leaves. The walls of the vestibule are set with niches for statuary.

The chamber itself is rectangular, and is 112 feet long by 82 in width, and 30 feet in height. The ceiling is entirely of cast iron, deeply paneled, with stained glass skylights, and ornamented in the richest style with foliage, pendants, and drops. The hall is surrounded by a gallery capable of seating one thousand persons. A portion of the gallery, over the chair of the Vice-President, is appropriated to reporters for the press. A section of the gallery, in front of the chair, is also reserved for the use of the diplomatic corps. The Secretary of the Senate, and his two assistants, occupy a desk immediately in front of the chair, and at the foot of this desk sit the special reporters of the debates. The seats of the Senators are ranged in three semicircular rows fronting the chair, each being supplied with a small desk standing in front of it. The walls and ceiling are painted in very high colors, and the iron-work bronzed and gilded. The chamber is lighted at night by gas, above the skylights, and is of such an even temper that it can scarcely be distinguished from daylight. The galleries are reached by magnificent marble staircases at either end of the hall, ceiled with ornamental iron-work, and lighted by stained glass skylights. These staircases, and those corresponding in the south wing, are the most striking points of architecture in the extension. The Senate chamber is surrounded by a corridor, which separates it from the Secretary's office and committee-rooms ranged around the outer walls of the wing.

Immediately in the rear of the chair is the Senators' Retiring Room, 38 by 21½ feet, and 19½ in height. This is one of the gems of the building. The ceiling is of white marble, deeply paneled, and supported by four

fluted columns of highly polished Italian marble. The
walls are of Tennessee marble, in which are set huge
plate-glass mirrors, serving for panels.

Adjoining the retiring-room, on the west, is the President's Room, which he occupies when attending to business in Congress. It is a square room, beautifully ceiled
with frescoed representations, typical of the history of the
country. On the walls, which are superbly decorated with
arabesques in secco, are to be seen portraits of the first
President and his Cabinet, executed by Costantino Brumidi.

The Vice-President's Room adjoins the retiring-room
on the east, and is also highly ornamented, and contains a
large portrait of Washington, by Rembrandt Peale. The
Reception Room and Senate Post Office are entered from
the vestibule, and are also beautiful apartments, with
walls decorated in secco painting, and gilded and frescoed ceilings.

Two staircases leading to the basement, are ornamented with richly-foliated bronze railings, decorated with
figures of the eagle, the deer, and Cupids. The basement
contains a suite of committee-rooms, mostly ornamented
in fresco and distemper, in the Italian and Pompeian
styles. The corridors are exquisitely ornamented in distemper, by Signor Brumidi; the designs in arabesque
and panel-work being taken from the loggia of Raphael
and the ruins of Pompeii. These minutely-finished paintings embody illustrations of the natural history of
America, the ornithology being mostly painted from the
life. The corridors and rooms of both stories are paved
with encaustic tiles laid in mosaic, after the choicest pat-
terns of Pompeian and modern design, and are lighted by
gorgeous bronze chandeliers.

The Hall of Representatives.—This hall is in the centre of the south wing, and is situated precisely like the Senate chamber, but larger in its proportions, and more gaudily painted and ornamented. It is 139 feet long, 93 feet wide, and 30 feet high, with a gallery running entirely around the hall, affording seats for 1,200 persons. Sections of the gallery are railed off for the especial use of the diplomatic corps and the reporters for the press. The reporters for the government have a desk directly below the chair of the Speaker. The elaborate ceiling of iron, supported by trusses from the roof, is paneled with glass to light the hall, each panel being ornamented by the arms of a State, represented in stained glass. The casting for the ceilings for both halls of Congress, is the work of Janes, Beebe & Co. The painting was done by German and Italian artists. The hall is surrounded by a corridor, outside of which is a range of committee-rooms, and offices of the Clerk of the House. The Speaker's Room is immediately in the rear of his chair, across the private lobby, and is highly decorated with mirrors and paintings, as are all the principal rooms in this wing. The main entrance from the portico will be occupied by double doors of bronze, richly ornamented with historical representations in bas-relief, designed by Rogers, and cast in Munich. Adjoining the grand colonnaded vestibule of the entrance from the eastern portico, is the House Post Office. The ascent to the gallery is by two grand marble staircases at the ends of the hall, like those in the Senate wing. There are also two staircases descending from the southern lobby of the House into the basement, with bronze railings of the same pattern as those in the north wing.

The basement is occupied by committee and document rooms. The room of the Committee on Agriculture is particularly beautiful; the walls and ceiling are painted in fresco, by Signor Brumidi. The arched ceiling is divided into four compartments, in which are represented the four seasons: in the eastern division, Flora is scattering Spring flowers; in the southern, Ceres holds full sheaves of grain; in the western, Bacchus revels in the products of the vine; and in the northern division, Boreas is accompanied by fierce winds and rains. On the eastern wall is a fresco of the call of Cincinnatus from the plough to the dictatorship; and upon the opposite wall is a companion painting of Putnam called from the plough to the battle of Lexington.

The basement is traversed, north and south, by a corridor 24½ feet broad, containing thirty monolithic fluted columns of white marble, with capitals foliated with tobacco leaves and buds, supporting a ceiling of cast-iron panels. This corridor extends the entire length of the Capitol, terminating with a door at each end of the basement story.

The Supreme Court Room.—The hall occupied by the court was formerly the Senate chamber, and has been used by the court since December, 1860. It is situated upon the eastern side of the north wing of the centre building; is semicircular, 75 feet long by 45 in height to the apex of the domed ceiling, which is paneled with stuccoed mouldings. A screen of Ionic columns, of green breccia or Potomac marble, supports a gallery upon the eastern side of the hall. The bench of the judges is ranged in front of the colonnade, facing the semicircle occupied by the bar and the lobby for spectators. Attached to the wall opposite the bench are consoles, supporting the busts of the former Chief Justices—John Jay, John Rutledge, Oliver Ellsworth, and John Marshall. The main entrance to the hall is from the corridor connecting the two houses of Congress.

The Library of Congress.—The library, when completed, will embrace the entire western projection of the centre building. It is situated on the west of the rotunda, and opens upon a portico of ten coupled columns, fronting upon the western park and the city, commanding a charming view of the Potomac dotted with white sails, and the green hills of Virginia rising gently in the distance.

The main room is 91 feet long, 34 feet wide, and 38 feet high, and is fitted up with three stories of iron cases, each nine feet six inches high. The lower story consists of alcoves nine feet wide, projecting eight feet six inches from the wall, with seven shelves, graduated in height. The second story has similar alcoves, with a projection of five feet. The wall of the third story is lined with cases without projections. The galleries are continued across the ends of the room, where they are supported by brackets. The galleries are floored with cast-iron plates, and protected by pedestals and railings, and are reached by semicircular staircases recessed in the end walls. The ceiling is of iron, skylighted with ground glass, and rests upon twenty-four massive foliated brackets of iron, weighing a ton each. The pilasters and panels are tastefully ornamented, and the whole is painted a delicate cream color. The railings are bronzed, and the points and drops

7*

are burnished with gold leaf. The room is lighted by five windows in front, besides the skylights. The library was designed by Mr. Walter, and the castings executed by Janes, Beebe & Co.

The purchase of books for the library was commenced under the act of Congress of April 24, 1800, at the suggestion of Mr. Jefferson. That act appropriated $5,000 for the purpose, to be expended by the Secretary of the Senate and the Clerk of the House of Representatives, under the direction of a joint committee of both houses. By an act of January 26, 1802, the President of the Senate and the Speaker of the House, for the time being, were authorized to establish such regulations and restrictions in relation to the use of the library as they might deem proper; and, from time to time, to alter or amend the same. By the same act, the President of the United States was authorized to appoint a librarian to take charge of the library. The collection, amounting to about 3,000 volumes, was consumed in the north wing of the Capitol when it was burned by the British, on the 24th of August, 1814.

In view of this loss, Mr. Jefferson offered his own private library to Congress, and on the 21st of October, 1814, the Committee on the Library was authorized to make the purchase, and having agreed upon the terms, on the 31st of January, 1815, an appropriation of $23,950 was made for that purpose. The books, numbering about 7,500, were transferred to the city of Washington, and placed in the Post Office building, where Congress was then sitting. The library was removed from thence, in 1818, to the Capitol, and located in a small room over the hall now occupied by the Supreme Court. Upon the completion of the centre of the Capitol, in 1825, the library was removed to its present location.

On the 24th of December, 1851, the library, then numbering 55,000 volumes, was partially destroyed by fire, which was accidentally communicated from a defective flue in the adjoining masonry; 20,000 volumes, occupying a detached apartment, were saved, and among them, fortunately, was a large portion of the collection purchased of Mr. Jefferson.

Temporary accommodations were immediately prepared, and $10,000 appropriated for a commencement of the restoration of the books destroyed. By an act of March 19, 1852, an appropriation of $72,500 was made for the repair of the library room, and the present beautiful structure was completed and furnished, ready for occupation, on July 1, 1853. An appropriation of $75,000 was made, August 31, 1852, to meet the expense of the extraordinary purchase of books necessary to restore the library to its former state.

An annual appropriation of $5,000 is made for the purchase of miscellaneous books, and $2,000 for law books. Selections are carefully made from the best bibliographical and literary authorities, under the superintendence of the Joint Committee on the Library. The purchase of law books is directed by the judges of the Supreme Court of the United States, in accordance with an act of Congress of July 14, 1832.

The library is general in selection, but is particularly full upon politics and international and civil law. The collection now numbers 70,000 volumes, exclusive of documents,—which are kept in separate libraries of the Senate and House, and number about 80,000 volumes, including duplicates. The classification of the books, upon the shelves and in the catalogue, is the one adopted by Jefferson, and based upon Lord Bacon's division of learning. A complete and critical catalogue is now in press and nearly ready for publication.

According to the regulations established by the President of the Senate and Speaker of the House, the library is kept open every week-day during the sessions of Congress, from 9 o'clock A. M. until 3 P. M., and for the same hours on Tuesdays, Thursdays, and Saturdays during the recess. The use of the library is limited, by acts of Congress, to the President of the United States, the Vice-President, members of the Senate and House of Representatives, Judges of the Supreme Court, Cabinet officers, the Diplomatic corps, the Secretary of the Senate, Clerk of the House of Representatives, and Agent of the Joint Committee on the Library.

The Law Library.—In the basement, directly under the hall of the Supreme Court, in the room formerly occupied by the court, is the Law Department of the Library of Congress, which is separated from the main library for the convenience of the court. The room is of the same dimensions as the hall above, though less in height. The massive arches rest upon Doric columns, and the semicircular wall is studded with alcoves, containing 16,000 volumes of law ; forming the choicest and most extensive collection upon the subject in America. It is particularly rich in works upon the civil, maritime, and commercial law. A complete catalogue was published in December, 1860.

The Old Hall of Representatives.—The magnificent

hall formerly occupied by the House of Representatives, is situated in the south wing of the centre building, between the rotunda and the present hall of the House. This stately hall is one of the most interesting relics of the history of Congress. The grand and imposing architecture still remains firm, like the Constitution, bidding defiance, as it were, to all change. It is semicircular in form, 95 feet in length, and 60 feet in height to the apex of the vaulted ceiling. Twenty-four massive Corinthian columns, of variegated green breccia, support the entablature, from which springs the domed ceiling, beautifully painted in panel to imitate that of the Pantheon at Rome. From the centre of the ceiling rises a handsomely painted cupola, through which the light is admitted. In the tympanum of the arch stands a colossal statue of Liberty, modeled in plaster, by Signor Causici. Beneath this figure, upon the entablature, is the American eagle, modeled from life, and cut in sandstone, by Signor Valaperti. Over the main entrance from the rotunda, is a beautiful statue, by Franzoni, representing History standing in a winged car, the wheel of which, resting on a globe, forms the face of a clock. The figure lends a listening ear, and, with pen and volume in hand, seems about to record the events as time rolls on. A full-length portrait of Lafayette adorns the western wall of the hall,—a present to Congress on the occasion of his visit to the United States, in 1825. The opposite wall bears a full-length portrait of Washington, painted by Vanderlyn, by order of Congress, for which he received $2,500.

The Speaker's chair and desks have been removed, and the grand corridor traverses the hall to the south wing. The galleries, occupying the space between the columns and the wall, are to be removed, and the floor laid with tessellated pavement, when the hall will form an open court, serving as an additional rotunda, and as a receptacle for historical paintings and sculpture.

The Document Library of the House.—This library occupies very incommodious apartments situated in the second story of the old south wing, and is reached by a flight of stairs at the left of the entrance of the old hall of Representatives. It contains about 65,000 volumes of documents, laws, reports, debates, and newspapers, and is accessible to members of Congress, and persons introduced by them. The library is to be removed to more suitable and convenient apartments in the south wing. It is in charge of a librarian appointed by the Clerk of the House.

The Commissioner of Public Buildings.—This officer has in charge the care of the public buildings in the city, the public parks and grounds, and all streets and avenues under the control of the government. He is appointed by the President, whom it is customary for him to serve in the capacity of usher at receptions and on occasions of ceremony. The Commissioner is assisted in his other duties by clerks, and occupies apartments on the west front of the basement story of the centre building of the Capitol.

The Court of Claims.—This court occupies rooms upon the basement story of the centre building of the Capitol, on the western front. The formation and duties of the court will be included in the chapter on the judicial department of the government.

The Capitol Grounds.—The Capitol is skirted on the western front by a stone terrace twenty-five feet wide, from which the glacis is descended by a double flight of stone steps to a second terrace or embankment, from which a second flight of steps leads to the sloping park below. These grounds are traversed by three flagged walks, fifteen feet wide, diverging from the foot of the first flight of steps and terminating at heavy stone gateways in the lofty iron palisade which surrounds the park. This park is ornamented with flower-beds and graveled walks, and a fountain in the centre, throwing a jet one hundred feet in height.

In the eastern park is a colossal statue of Washington, executed in marble by Horatio Greenough. He is represented sitting in a curule chair, his body nude to the waist, the right arm and lower limbs being draped. In his left hand he presents a Roman sword, hilt foremost, while with his right he points to heaven. The statue rests upon a pedestal of granite, twelve feet high, upon which is inscribed, "George Washington, First in War, First in Peace, and First in the Hearts of his Countrymen." This statue is evidently an imitation of the antique statue of Jupiter Tonans. The ancients made their statues of Jupiter naked above and draped below, as being visible to the gods but invisible to men. This is eminently the case with this statue, being sufficiently exposed to the heavens, but scarcely recognizable, in this garb, to his countrymen.

The Capitol Guard.—The Capitol is protected by a vigilant police force, whose duty is to keep the peace and preserve order in and about the building and grounds, by day and night. There is a guard-room in the basement, in which disturbers of the peace are temporarily confined, as occasion requires. The guard extend civilities, at all times, to strangers, and direct them to the different parts of the Capitol. They are easily distinguished by their badge.

CONGRESS.

The old Continental Congress and Congress of the Confederation, was composed of delegates sent from the colonies to discuss the grievances charged against the mother-country, and to resolve upon measures of redress. The first session was held at Carpenters' Hall, Philadelphia, September 5, 1774. The following sessions commenced at Philadelphia, May 10, 1775; Baltimore, December 20, 1776; Philadelphia, March 4, 1777; Lancaster, Penn., September 27, 1777; York, Penn., September 30, 1777; Philadelphia, July 2, 1778; Princeton, N. J., June 30, 1783; Annapolis, Md., November 26, 1783; Trenton, N. J., November 1, 1784; New York City, January 11, 1785, where the session continued until August 12, 1790.

The Congress of the United States of America, under the Constitution, assembled for the first time, March 4, 1789, and on July 16, 1790, passed an act locating the present seat of government, with the provision that Congress should sit in Philadelphia until the seat of government should be removed; and Congress commenced its first session in the Capitol, in the city of Washington, November 17, 1800.

All legislative powers are vested, by the Constitution, in Congress, which consists of a Senate and House of Representatives, and must assemble at least once a year, on the first Monday in December, unless they shall by law appoint a different day. The second session of every

Congress terminates, by law, at twelve o'clock at noon, of the 4th of March next following the commencement of the session. A majority of each house constitutes a quorum to do business, but a smaller number may adjourn from day to day. Neither house can adjourn for more than three days without consent of the other. Senators and Representatives are bound by oath to support the Constitution. Members of both houses are privileged from arrest, except for treason, felony, or breach of the peace.

The Senate.—The Senate is composed of two Senators from each State, chosen by the legislature for six years. In case of a vacancy, the Governor of the State appoints until the next meeting of the legislature. No person can be a Senator under thirty years of age, or who has not been nine years a citizen of the United States, and is not at the time of election an inhabitant of the State for which he is chosen. The Vice-President is President of the Senate, but has no vote except on an equal division, when he has the casting-vote. On the motion of a Senator, the galleries may be cleared, and the doors closed for secret session. The Senate held their sessions with closed doors until the second session of the third Congress, when they decided to sit with open doors and galleries, and to allow the debates to be reported, except on occasions when secrecy is required by law, or thought advisable. Twelve o'clock at noon is the hour for meeting, unless otherwise ordered. The Secretary of the Senate, the Sergeant-at-arms, Doorkeeper, and Assistant-doorkeepers, are chosen on the second Monday of the first session of each Congress. The Vice-President does not participate in debate.

The House of Representatives.—This body is composed of members chosen every second year by the people of the States, and each is required to be twenty-five years of age, seven years a citizen of the United States, and an inhabitant of the State in which he is chosen. The apportionment of Representatives to population is made every ten years, after taking the census, the whole number being divided by 233, the number to which the House is limited by law, gives the rate of representation to population. There may be a greater number of Representatives when new States are admitted between the periods of the census. Delegates from Territories have a seat upon the floor, and a voice in debate, but no vote. The Speaker and officers of the House are chosen by the House for the Congress. The privileges of the Speaker are the same as those of any other Representative. The House meets at twelve o'clock at noon, unless otherwise specially ordered.

Committees.—The appointment of committees of the two Houses is by the Vice-President and Speaker, respectively. To these committees is confided the initiation of business. The chairman of each committee reports, by bill or otherwise, and upon such report the Senate or House goes into Committee of the Whole House, when all the members are regarded as forming one committee. The Speaker calls a member to take the chair. The Speaker is then allowed to participate in debate. The Vice-President does not leave the chair. After consideration of the subject before the committee, it rises, and the chairman reports the action of the committee to the House or Senate.

CHAPTER V.

THE JUDICIAL DEPARTMENT.

THE judicial powers of the government are vested in a Supreme Court and such inferior courts as Congress may from time to time establish. The present establishment consists of a Supreme Court, Circuit Courts, District Courts, and Court of Claims.

THE SUPREME COURT.

This court consists of a Chief Justice and eight Associates, appointed by the President, to hold their offices during good behavior, any five of whom shall be a quorum, and hold annually one session, commencing on the first Monday in December. The court has exclusive jurisdiction of all controversies of a civil nature, where a State is a party, except between a State and its citizens, and except also between a State and citizens of other States, or aliens,—in which latter case it has original, but not exclusive jurisdiction. It has, exclusively, all such jurisdiction of suits or proceedings against ambassadors as a court can have, by the law of nations. The trial of issues in fact, are by jury. This court has appellate jurisdiction from the Circuit and State courts, in certain cases provided for by law. Each justice is also judge of one of the circuit courts. The officers of the court are, the Attorney-General, a clerk, deputy-clerk, reporter, marshal, and crier. Attorneys and counselors admitted to the bar of the court, must have practiced three years in the supreme court of the State in which they reside, and must have a fair private and professional character. They must take the oath to support the law and the Constitution. The court, in term-time, sits daily · from 11 A. M. to 3 P. M.

THE ATTORNEY-GENERAL.

By act of Congress, September 24th, 1789, a person learned in the law is appointed to act as Attorney-General of the United States, sworn to a faithful execution of his office. It is his duty to prosecute and conduct all suits in the Supreme Court in which the United States are concerned, and give his advice upon questions of law, when required by the President, or when requested by the heads of any of the departments, touching any matters that may concern their departments. He is a Cabinet officer, and meets the President and Secretaries in council. He is allowed an assistant, three clerks, and a messenger.

THE COURT OF CLAIMS.

This court was established February 24th, 1855, and consists of three judges, appointed by the President, by and with the consent of the Senate. Any two of the judges constitute a quorum. They hold their offices during good behavior, and hear and determine all claims founded upon any law of Congress, or upon any regulation of an executive department, or upon any contract, express or implied, with the government, which may be referred to the court by either house of Congress. A solicitor, and two assistant-solicitors, to represent the government before the court, are appointed by the President by and with the consent of the Senate. The court keeps a record of its proceedings, and reports to Congress at the commencement of each session, and monthly during the session. There is a clerk, an assistant-clerk, and messenger attached to and appointed by the court. Sessions are held during the time of session of Congress, and during the remainder of the year, when there is any business on the docket. Court days are from Monday until Thursday, and Friday, on pressing occasions. Saturday is occupied by the judges as a day of conference.

CHAPTER VI.

GOVERNMENTAL AND NATIONAL ESTABLISHMENTS.

THERE are certain important establishments and institutions at the seat of government, which, for the sake of preserving a reasonable unity of our theme, we have preferred to classify under the designation given to this chapter. Some of them, indeed, are nominally branches of the executive departments, while others are either related to the government by their subjection to its oversight, or by their identity with national interests.

WASHINGTON NAVY YARD.

During the administration of President Jefferson, the Navy Yard situated in the District of Columbia was established by an act of Congress, approved March 27th,

1804. It is enclosed on the landward sides by a brick wall, the fourth side fronting the Anacostia river. Entering the yard through a handsome gateway, designed by Benjamin Latrobe, the visitor is greeted with the sight of trophies of naval warfare. These consist of cannon captured by our gallant seamen, not the least interesting amongst them being the two whose history is recorded in the inscription borne by one of them : " On the 3d day of August, 1804, Captain Stephen Decatur, in command of an American gun-boat off Tripoli, boarded and captured in succession two Tripolitan gun-boats, armed with this and the adjacent gun." The Navy Yard covers about thirty-seven acres of land ; and, besides the workshops, contains the officers' quarters. The main building is 432 feet in length on the east and west fronts, and 265 feet in length on the north and south fronts ; it contains the boiler-shop, machine-shop, pattern-shop, smithery, and erecting-shop. Another large building is situated eastward of the main building ; it contains the forge-shop,— in which may be seen in operation a steam-hammer weighing five tons,—the anchor and faggoting shops. The business of the latter is to convert the scrap-iron collected from various Navy Yards into blooms, from which the heaviest anchors are forged. Northward of the first-mentioned building is the iron-foundry, 265 feet long and 65 feet wide, in which all the castings are made for the machinery of government ships, and the shot and shells for the Ordnance Department are cast. The new Ordnance building, which is about the same size, is seen to the westward. The Dahlgren guns, howitzers. carriages, Minie balls, and various forms of cartridges, are here manufactured, under careful supervision. Besides these, there are various other buildings for offices, carpenters, blockmakers, pyrotechnists, riggers, copper-rolling mill, navy stores, brass-foundry, camboose-shop, and tank-shop. In the southeast corner of the yard is the ship-house and marine railway.

UNITED STATES COAST SURVEY.

The office of this important enterprise is situated on New Jersey avenue. Although the service of surveying the Atlantic, Gulf, and Pacific coasts of the United States is legally under the control of the Treasury Department, its duties are discharged by officers of the army and navy, with the assistance of scientific civilians. The work of survey is divided into nine sections, each of which commences by measuring a base-line five or ten miles in length; this is performed by using a compensating base-apparatus, and requires the greatest care and exactness. After this a series of stations is established, and by computing the triangulation of these from the principal base, a centre is obtained for all subsequent measurements. The topography being completed, the hydrographer commences to take soundings. When the field-work is finished, the results thus obtained are forwarded to the office in Washington, where the drawings are reduced, engraved, electrotyped and printed. .

NATIONAL OBSERVATORY.

The National Observatory is situated southwest of the Executive Mansion, upon an elevated site, commanding a beautiful view of the noble Potomac river, and in full sight of the two cities of Washington and Georgetown. It was originally designed and used for a hydrographical office. The preparation of wind and current charts, the regulation of chronometers, and the other branches of hydrographical research still occupy the principal care of the Observatory, in which astronomical investigation is made a secondary consideration. In the west wing of the building is placed the transit instrument, under a slit twenty inches wide, extending across the roof, and down the wall of the apartment on each side to within four or five feet of the floor.

The transit instrument is a seven-foot achromatic with a clear aperture of 5.3 inches, and was made by Ertel & Son, of Munich; the mounting consists of two granite piers, seven feet high, each formed of a solid block of that stone, let down below the floor and imbedded in a stone foundation eight feet deep, and completely isolated from the building. Midway between the piers, and running north and south, is the artificial horizon, composed of a slab of granite ten feet long, nineteen inches deep, and thirteen inches broad; it rests on the foundation, and is isolated from the floor, with the level of which the top of it is even, with a space all around it of half an inch; in the middle of this slab, and in the nadir of the telescope, there is a mortise, nine inches square and ten inches deep, in which the artificial horizon is placed to protect it from the wind during the adjustment for collimation, or the determination of the error of collimation of level, and the adjustment for stellar focus, verticality of wires, and the other uses of the collimating eye-piece. Besides this delicate instrument, and connected with its uses, there is an astronomical clock to denote sidereal time, the electric chronograph, invented by Professor John Locke. In the south wing of the building is the prime vertical transit,

8

and the photograph-room. A very fine library of astronomical works, and a normal clock, made by Kessels, of Altona, are in the room of the Superintendent. The clock has a gridiron pendulum, and its annual variation is less than eleven seconds. In the east wing is the mural circle. Here also is the meridian circle ; the telescope tube is 56 inches in length, the object-glass has 4.5 inches of clear aperture, and 58.2 of focal length. The electric clock, by which chronometers are regulated, is worthy of observation, as well as the valuable collection of charts. In the library, amongst many other rare works, are to be found a number of star charts, and a daily record of the barometer, thermometer, state of the winds and of the heavens, compiled by Le Verrier, from observations extending from Algiers to St. Petersburg in latitude, and from Constantinople to Paris in longitude. The large equatorial in the dome was constructed by Merz & Mahler, of Munich, and is a counterpart of the instruments at Dorpat and Berlin. The object-glass of this instrument has a clear aperture of 9.65 inches, and a focal length of 14 feet 4.3 inches ; its magnifying power ranges from 80 to 600, although the higher power is seldom attained, owing to the fact that the slightest tremor of the building throws the object out of the focal plane. When required, a clockwork motion is attached to compensate for the revolution of the earth upon its axis. An electric chronograph is also connected with it when it is used as a transit instrument. The observatory is open to visitors every day between the hours of 9 A. M. and 3 P. M., and a courteous officer renders all necessary assistance, and furnishes all needful information.

THE WASHINGTON NATIONAL MONUMENT.

The subject of erecting a national monument to Washington was mooted by the Continental Congress, as early as 1783, when a resolution was passed ordering a statue to be erected "in honor of George Washington, the illustrious Commander-in-chief of the United States of America during the war which vindicated and secured their liberty, sovereignty, and independence." The commissioners who laid out the city set apart the present site of the monument, but for want of funds, the statue was not ordered. The ground selected by the commissioners was marked on the plan of the city submitted to Congress by Washington in 1793, and Washington died in the belief that on that spot he would be commemorated.

In 1799, Congress passed a resolution authorizing President Adams to correspond with Mrs. Washington, asking her consent to the removal and interment of her husband's remains beneath a monument to be erected by the government in the Capitol. Mrs. Washington consented, in the following beautiful and concise letter :—

Taught, by the great example I have so long had before me, never to oppose my private wishes to the public will, I must consent to the request of Congress which you had the goodness to transmit to me; and, in doing this, I need not—I cannot—say what a sacrifice of individual feeling I make to a sense of public duty.

The monument was not erected, and Washington's remains were therefore not removed.

In 1800, a bill passed one house of Congress, for erecting a " mausoleum of American granite and marble, in a pyramidal form, one hundred feet square at the base, and of a proportional height." In 1816, the subject was again discussed without effect. Congress again made an application, in 1832, to the proprietors of Mount Vernon, for the removal and deposit of the remains of Washington in the Capitol, in conformity with the resolution of 1799. The legislature of Virginia protested against the movement, and Mr. John A. Washington declined the proposal.

On the 26th of September, 1833, several citizens of Washington assembled together, and in the course of a series of meeting, digested a plan for erecting a national monument. An organization was formed, styled the Washington National Monument Society, and Chief Justice John Marshall was chosen president. Since the death of Judge Marshall, the successive Presidents of the United States have held that position, by the constitution of the society.

Subscriptions, limited to one dollar, were immediately commenced, for raising the requisite funds; and this system being found inadequate, in 1846 the donations were made unlimited, but the collection still increased very slowly. It became necessary to decide upon a plan for the edifice, and from a large number of designs, mostly fantastic and ill conceived, that of Robert Mills was finally selected, consisting of an Egyptian obelisk, six hundred feet in height, surrounded by a Doric colonnade called a pantheon, to contain statues and revolutionary relics. The site of the monument was set apart by the President of the United States, under an act of Congress of January 21, 1848, and covers thirty acres of ground, near the Potomac, directly west of the Capitol and south of the President's mansion, commanding a full view of the river. It is at the intersection of Louisiana and

Virginia avenues, upon the Mall, and is called Monument Square.

The corner-stone was laid July 4, 1848. At ten o'clock that morning, a grand military, civic, and Masonic procession was formed at the City Hall, under the direction of Mr. Joseph H. Bradley, Marshal of the day; the military being under the command of Major-General Quitman. Included in the procession were delegations from several tribes of Indians. The line formed eight abreast, numbering about four thousand, and marched to the Monument Square, with banners flying, martial music, and the solemn tolling of the bells of the city. Hon. Robert C. Winthrop, the orator of the day, delivered an eloquent oration upon the life and character of Washington. His peroration contained the following beautiful language :—

Let the column which we are about to construct, be at once a pledge and an emblem of perpetual union! Let the foundations be laid, let the superstructure be built up and cemented, let each stone be raised and riveted, in a spirit of national brotherhood! And may the earliest ray of the rising sun—till that sun shall set to rise no more—draw forth from it daily, as from the fabled statue of antiquity, a strain of national harmony, which shall strike a responsive cord in every heart throughout the Republic!

Proceed, then, fellow-citizens, with the work for which you have assembled! Lay the corner-stone of a monument which shall adequately bespeak the gratitude of the whole American People to the illustrious Father of his Country! Build it to the skies: you cannot outreach the loftiness of his principles! Found it upon the massive and eternal rock: you cannot make it more enduring than his fame! Construct it of the peerless Parian marble: you cannot make it purer than his life! Exhaust upon it the rules and principles of ancient and modern art: you cannot make it more proportionate than his character!

* * * * The Republic may perish; the wide
arch of our ranged Union may fall; star by star its glories
may expire; stone after stone its columns and its capital
may moulder and crumble; all other names which adorn
its annals may be forgotten; but as long as human hearts
shall anywhere pant, or human tongues shall anywhere
plead, for a true, rational, constitutional liberty, those
hearts shall enshrine the memory, and those tongues shall
prolong the fame, of George Washington.

The Grand Master then delivered an appropriate Masonic address, after which the Fraternity entered, beneath
a beautifully decorated arch, to the excavation, where the
Grand Master of Masons laid the corner-stone, with the
usual ceremonies. The stone, weighing twelve tons, had
been prepared with a cavity lined with zinc, into which
the inscription plate was placed, together with about one
hundred other articles, consisting of books, portraits,
maps, newspapers, coins and medals, Masonic records,
and the design of the monument. The Grand Master wore
the apron and used the gavel with which Washington laid
the corner-stone of the Capitol. The inscription upon the
plate was as follows:

4TH JULY, 1776,

DECLARATION OF INDEPENDENCE OF THE UNITED STATES OF
AMERICA.

4TH JULY, 1848,

THIS CORNER-STONE LAID, OF A MONUMENT, BY THE PEOPLE
OF THE UNITED STATES, TO GEORGE WASHINGTON.

The names of the officers of the society were also inscribed on the plate. The ceremony of the day was closed
by a brilliant display of fire-works in the evening.

The foundation of the monument is solid rock. The
base of the shaft is 81 feet square, and the shaft is to rise

to the height of 600 feet, and to be encircled by a grand colonnade or pantheon, 250 feet in diameter and 100 feet high; over the portico of which is a colossal statue of Washington, 30 feet high, in a chariot drawn by six horses, driven by Victory, all of colossal proportions. The colonnade is to consist of 30 columns, 12 feet in diameter and 45 feet high, surrounded by an entablature of 20 feet, and a balustrade 15 feet in height. The entablature will be decorated with the arms of the States, inclosed in wreaths of bronze. The portico consists of a projection supported by four columns, and is reached by a grand flight of marble steps. Over the centre of the portico will be emblazoned the arms of the United States. The interior, or rotunda, will be ornamented with statues of the signers of the Declaration of Independence, set in niches in the surrounding wall; and upon the wall, above the niches, will be represented, in basso-relievo, the principal battles of the Revolution. Conspicuous in front of the entrance of the rotunda, will stand a statue of Washington. Within the stylobate or base of the monument, will be a labyrinth of apartments arranged in a most intricate manner.

The material of which the facing of the monument is constructed, is what is known as Symington's large crystal marble, procured from the vicinity of Baltimore. The body of the wall is of blue gneiss. The interior lining is to be decorated with blocks presented by the different States and foreign nations, societies and city corporations, ornamented with coats of arms and appropriate inscriptions, and so disposed in the wall as to be visible in ascending the shaft of the monument. The ascent will be by a spiral iron staircase, lighted with gas,—the only openings, except the doors below, being star-shaped windows near the top. It is proposed to close the apex with a cone of glass. Besides the staircase, the ascent will be made by means of machinery up the centre of the shaft. The present height of the structure is 184 feet. It is to be hoped that more active measures will be taken, and that the plan will be carried out by the government; as that is the only proper and effective method of securing the necessary means for its completion.

The United States has not yet reached the age of monument-building. This nation has not even emerged from the youth of action into the prime of its history, and has yet to run a long and brilliant career before it shall pass into a dotage of inactivity, when it can afford to rest upon the laurels of the past. It can then spend its second childhood in recording the annals of gathered glories, and in erecting splendid monuments over the ashes of departed merit. When our wealth and population shall have increased, and the federal and democratic spirit of the present shall have yielded to the sway of interest, and an inevitable aristocracy; then an austere administration will possess the power and means of dedicating magnificent memorials to the merit of which the age will find itself most in need.

The great monuments of other nations have all been erected at government expense, and at the will of despotic rulers. The pyramids of Egypt would never have been built by voluntary subscription. The Dacian victories of Trajan would have remained uncommemorated, if his pictured column had awaited the denarii of the Roman people. The column of Antonine, the triumphal arches of the Roman emperors, the Hotel des Invalides, and all great monuments, have been government works. The Peter-pence for the stupendous monument to the original of apostolic succession, were also collected under a peremptory tax; the subscription for the Nelson monument, barely sufficed for the admission fee of the proposed memorial into Westminster Abbey. We can scarcely expect to be more successful in the United States, and deserve little reproach on account of the fact that, in a few years, we have not succeeded in perpetuating, in brass and stone, the memory of Washington. His glory is so fresh in the appreciation of his countrymen, that they neglect the importance of securing to posterity an enduring record of their veneration. The work should not depend upon casual contributions, but be completed immediately at the expense of the government.

When this national memorial shall raise its head towards heaven, a tower of strength amid the clouds and tempests which environ it, and when the sun shines out upon it in the calm repose of its majesty, it will then become a fitting symbol of the great hero and sage, first in war and first in peace, " *adversis major par secundis.*"

SMITHSONIAN INSTITUTION.

It will be observed that we have designated the contents of this chapter as descriptive of governmental and national establishments, as distinct from the topics belonging to the former chapters upon the executive, legislative, and judicial departments. We were led to this choice by the consideration that there are, in the federal city, certain institutions which are national, both in their objects and organization, and, in a greater or less degree,

8*

under the patronage or control of the national Government, or else deserving of national recognition.

The Smithsonian Institution is so far identified with the Government, that while it involves the nation in no expense, except perhaps for printing, the fund from which its income is derived belongs to the people of the United States, in trust for special purposes; and, with a view to the faithful discharge of that trust, the President of the United States, Vice-President, Chief Justice of the Supreme Court, Attorney-General, Secretaries of War, Navy, and Treasury, Postmaster-General, and Commissioner of Patents, are, *ex officio*, Regents of the Institution.

SMITHSONIAN INSTITUTION.

The building is situated on that portion of the public grounds extending westward from the capitol to the Potomac River, and known as the Mall. The style of architecture is the early Gothic, and a fine specimen of the richness of detail and ornamentation peculiar to the last half of the twelfth century, the transition period of architecture. It was designed by James Renwick, Jr., of New York, and is built of light-red sandstone obtained from the vicinity of Seneca Creek, a tributary of the Potomac, about twenty-three miles from Washington. The color of the stone harmonizes with the style of architecture, and produces a rich and solid effect.

The main building has, in the centre of its north front, two towers, of which the higher reaches an elevation of about 150 feet. On the south front is a tower, 37 feet square and 91 feet high. On the northeast corner is a campanile tower, 17 feet square and 117 feet high; at the southwest corner an octagonal tower, in which is a spiral staircase. There are nine towers in all.

The entire length of the building, from east to west, is 447 feet; its greatest breadth is 160 feet. The east wing is 82 by 52 feet, and $42\frac{1}{2}$ feet high to the top of its battlement; the west wing, including its projecting apsis, is 84 feet by 40, and 38 feet high; and each of the connecting ranges, including its cloister, is 60 feet by 49. The main building is 205 feet by 57, and, to the top of the corbel course, 58 feet high. The corner-stone was laid, with Masonic ceremonies, in the presence of President Polk, May 1st, 1847.

The founder of this Institution, James Smithson, was an Englishman, claiming a descent from the noble families of Northumberland and Somerset; until manhood he was known as James Lewis Macie, when he asserted his right to the family name of the Duke of Northumberland, and ever after called himself James Smithson. He possessed great scientific attainments and furnished many valuable memoirs for the Royal Society of England. After his decease, he bequeathed all his property—with a reservation of $25,000 to form the principal of an annuity for a relative—to the United States of America, " to found, at Washington, under the name of the Smithsonian Institution, an establishment FOR THE INCREASE AND DIFFUSION OF KNOWLEDGE AMONG MEN." The bequest having been legally tested by the High Court of Chancery in England, the United States, represented by Hon. Richard Rush, obtained a decree which placed them in possession of $515,169, which amount was placed in the Treasury of the United States, and has ever since remained intact,—the interest arising from it having been so judiciously husbanded as to furnish means for all the outlays for every purpose, including the cost of erecting its beautiful structure. The act incorporating the Institution was approved by the President, August 20, 1846, and the first session of the Board of Regents was commenced on the 7th of the following September. It was, however, principally occupied in discussions relative to the plan of organization, which was not adopted until the beginning of 1847. After full examination of various projects, the following programme of organization, presented by the Secretary, was decided upon as, in the opinion of the Regents, most nearly arriving at the intention of the founder :

To Increase Knowledge. It is proposed : 1. To stimulate men of talent to make original researches, by offering suitable rewards for memoirs containing new truths ; and, 2. To appropriate annually a portion of the income for particular researches, under the direction of suitable persons.

To Diffuse Knowledge. It is proposed: 1. To publish a series of periodical reports on the progress of the different branches of knowledge ; and,   2. To publish, occasionally, separate treatises on subjects of general interest.

Details of Plan to Incrase Knowledge.   I. By stimulating researches.   1. Facilities to be afforded for the production of original memoirs on all branches of knowledge.   2. The memoirs thus obtained to be published in a series of volumes, in a quarto form, and entitled Smithsonian Contributions to Knowledge.   3. No memoir, on subjects of physical science, to be accepted for publication, which does not furnish a positive addition to human knowledge, resting on original research ; and all unverified speculations to be rejected.   4. Each memoir presented to the Institution to be submitted for examination to a commission of persons of reputation for learning in the branch to which the memoir pertains, and to be accepted for publication only in case the report of this commission is favorable.   5. The commission to be chosen by the officers of the Institution, and the name of the author, as far as practicable, concealed, unless a favorable decision be made.   6. The volumes of the memoirs to be exchanged for the transactions of literary and scientific societies, and copies to be given to all the colleges, and principal libraries, in this country.   One part of the remaining copies may be offered for sale ; and the other carefully preserved, to form complete sets of the work, to supply the demand from new institutions.   7. An abstract, or popular account, of the contents of these memoirs to be given to the public through the annual report of the Regents to Congress.   II. By appropriating a part of the income, annually, to special objects of research, under the direction of suitable persons.   1. The objects, and the amount appropriated, to be recommended by counselors of the Institution.

2. Appropriations in different years to different objects;
so that in course of time each branch of knowledge may
receive a share.   3. The results obtained from these
appropriations to be published, with the memoirs before
mentioned, in the volumes of the Smithsonian Contributions to Knowledge.   4. Examples of objects for which
appropriations may be made: (1.) System of extended
meteorological observations for solving the problem of
American storms.   (2.) Explorations in descriptive natural history, and geological, magnetical, and topographical
surveys, to collect materials for the formation of a Physical Atlas of the United States.   (3.) Solution of experiment problems, such as a new determination of the
weight of the earth, of the velocity of electricity and of
light; chemical analyses of soils and plants; collection
and publication of scientific facts, accumulated in the
offices of government.   (4.) Institution of statistical inquiries with reference to physical, moral, and political
subjects.   (5.) Historical researches, and accurate surveys of places celebrated in American history.   (6.) Eth-
nological researches, particularly with reference to the
different races of men in North America; also, explorations and accurate surveys of the mounds and other
remains of the ancient people of our country.

Details of the Plan for Diffusing Knowledge.   I. By
the publication of a series of reports, giving an account
of the new discoveries in science, and of the changes made
from year to year in all branches of knowledge not
strictly professional.   1. These reports will diffuse a
kind of knowledge generally interesting, but which, at
present, is inaccessible to the public.   Some reports may
be published annually, others at longer intervals, as the

income of the Institution or the changes in the branches of knowledge may indicate. 2. The reports are to be prepared by collaborators eminent in the different branches of knowledge. 3. Each collaborator to be furnished with the journals and publications, domestic and foreign, necessary to the compilation of his report; to be paid a certain sum for his labors, and to be named on the title-page of the report. 4. The reports to be published in separate parts, so that persons interested in a particular branch can procure the parts relating to it without purchasing the whole. 5. These reports may be presented to Congress for partial distribution, the remaining copies to be given to literary and scientific institutions, and sold to individuals for a moderate price. II. By the publication of separate treatises on subjects of general interest. 1. These treatises may occasionally consist of valuable memoirs translated from foreign languages, or of articles prepared under the direction of the Institution, or procured by offering premiums for the best exposition of a given subject. 2. The treatises should, in all cases, be submitted to a commission of competent judges previous to their publication.

The only changes made in the policy above indicated have been the passage of resolutions, by the Regents, repealing the equal division of the income between the active operations and the museum and library, and further providing that the annual appropriations are to be apportioned specifically among the different objects and operations of the Institution, in such manner as may, in the judgment of the Regents, be necessary and proper for each, according to its intrinsic importance, and a compliance in good faith with the law.

An able writer in the Democratic Quarterly Review, published in Washington, February, 1861, cites the following responsible witnesses to establish the judicious manner in which the great work deputed to the Smithsonian Institution is performed:

" Professor Forbes, of Edinburg, in reference to a work of marine exploration, whose results have been given to the world at the charge of the Institution, observes : A more proper person than Professor Harvey, of the University of Dublin, could not have been selected for the elaboration of a ' Nereis Boreali-Americana;' and most honorable is it to the directors of the Smithsonian Institution of North America, that they should have selected this gentleman for the task of which we have now the first fruits. The trustees of that establishment are pursuing a course which is sure to do much towards the wholesome development of science in the United States. In the present instance, they have done what is both wise and generous ; and, in seeking the best man to do the difficult work they require done, have recognized nobly the truth that science belongs to the world, to all mankind, laboring for the benefit of all regions and races alike. And Professor Agassiz, in acknowledgment of services rendered him in the preparation of his important work on the Natural History of the United States, thus expresses himself: ' Above all, I must mention the Smithsonian Institution, whose officers, in the true spirit of its founder, have largely contributed to the advancement of my researches by forwarding to me for examination not only all the speciments of Testudinati collected for the museum of the Institution, but also those brought to Washington by the naturalists of the different parties that have explored the western Territories, or crossed the continent with the view of determining the best route for the Pacific railroad. These specimens have enabled me to determine the geographical distribution of this order of reptiles with a degree of precision which I could not have attained without this assistance.'"

We are indebted to the same writer, to whose comprehensive and well-condensed article we owe a grateful testimony, for calling our attention to the following important suggestions, contained in the eighth annual report of the Institution, prepared by Professor Henry :—

There is one part of the Smithsonian operations that attracts no public attention, though it is producing, it is believed, important results in the way of diffusing knowledge, and is attended, perhaps, with more labor than any other—the *scientific correspondence* of the Institution. Scarcely a day passes in which communications are not received from persons in different parts of the country, containing accounts of discoveries, which are referred to the Institution, or asking questions relative to some branch of knowledge. The rule was early adopted to give respectful attention to every letter received, and this has been faithfully adhered to from the beginning up to the present time. The ordinary inquiries addressed to the Secretary relate to the principles of mechanics, electricity, magnetism, meteorology, names of specimens of plants, minerals, insects, and, in short, to all objects or phenomena of a remarkable or unusual character. Requests are frequently made for lists of apparatus, for information as to the best books for the study of special subjects, hints for the organization of local societies, &c. Applications are also made by persons abroad for information relative to particular subjects respecting this country. When an immediate reply cannot be given to a question, the subject is referred by letter to some one of the Smithsonian co-laborers, to whose line of duty it pertains, and the answer is transmitted to the inquirer, either under the name of the person who gives the information, or that of the Institution, according to the circumstances of the case.

* * * * * * * * *

There is no country on the face of the earth in which knowledge is so generally diffused as in the United States; none in which there is more activity of mind or freedom of thought and discussion, and in which there is less regard to what should be considered as settled and well-established principles. It will not therefore be surprising that the Institution should be called upon to answer a great number of communications intended to subvert the present system of science, and to establish new and visionary conceptions in its stead; and that numerous letters should be received pertaining to such subjects as the quadrature of the circle, the trisection of the angle, the invention of self-moving machines, the creation of power, the overthrow of the Newtonian system of gravitation, and the invention of new systems of the universe.

Many of these communications are of such a character that, at first sight, it might seem best to treat them with silent neglect; but the rule has been adopted to state, candidly and respectfully, the objections to such propositions, and to endeavor to convince their authors that their ground is untenable.

In this Institution may be found the scientific results of the United States exploring expeditions, which are here preserved at the expense of the government, no other suitable place having as yet been prepared. This museum contains the best collection of specimens of natural history, and of foreign curiosities, to be found in America.

The Library of the Institution, already rich, promises to become the most valuable collection of scientific works in the world. In carrying out the plan of the Smithsonian Institution, it would be folly to expend any portion of its income in the purchase of works which could not forward

its settled policy; and no better proof can be afforded of
the efficiency of the managers of this great enterpise
than that the literary is made subordinate to, and considered the servant of, the scientific department.

We regret that it is not in our power to afford space
for a detailed description of the various scientific pursuits
which are prosecuted in the Institution, by competent persons, with an ardor that only science can inspire. The
following facts, gleaned from the report of 1856, and not
embracing the subsequent labors of the Institution, will
afford a faint idea of the accomplishments of an Institution which a large number of visitors suppose to be only
a national show-shop :—

A Library has been established, containing nearly
50,000 articles; a museum has been collected, the most
extensive in the world, as regards the natural history of the
North American Continent; a cabinet of apparatus has
been procured, through the liberality of Dr. Hare, and
other means of original research and illustration in the
principal phenomena of chemistry and natural philosophy;
lectures have been delivered annually, by some of the most
distinguished men in science and literature, before large
audiences; an extensive series of original papers on various branches of science has been published and distributed at the expense of the Institution, which has
also rendered aid in preparing them, by advances from its
funds, and the use of its library, collections, and influence;
natural history explorations have been made at the expense of the government, but principally at the instance
and under the scientific direction of this Institution, which
have done more to develop a knowledge of the peculiar
character of the western portions of this continent than

all previous researches on the subject; a system of exchange is now in successful operation, connecting in friendly relations the cultivators of literature and science in this country with their brethren in every part of the old world. A large amount of valuable material has been collected with regard to the meteorology of the North American continent, and a system of observations organized which, if properly conducted in future, will tend to establish a knowledge of the peculiarities of our climate, and to develop the laws of the storms which visit particularly the eastern portion of the United States during the winter. A series of original researches has also been made in the Institution in regard to different branches of natural history, and also to portions of physical science particularly applicable to economical purposes.

In leaving this branch of our theme, we desire to record our thanks to the Secretary and the scientific corps of the Institution for valuable aid, rendered with marked courtesy, in the preparation of this volume. For a detailed and accurate statement of the various objects of interest in the Institution, the reader is referred to a pamphlet prepared by Mr. W. J. Rhees, and sold by the attentive janitor.

The grounds surrounding the Smithsonian were laid out by A. J. Downing, who, at the time of his death, was devising an admirable system of improvements, which has not been subsequently prosecuted with much energy. A monument to his memory, erected by the American Pomological Society is placed conspicuously near the Institution, bearing the following inscriptions.

On the north side :—

THIS VASE

Was erected, by his Friends,

IN MEMORY OF

ANDREW JACKSON DOWNING,

Who died July 28, 1852, aged 37 years.

————

He was born, and lived,
And died, upon the Hudson River.
His life was devoted to the improvement of the national taste in
rural art,
an office for which his genius and the natural beauty amidst
which he lived had fully endowed him.
His success was as great as his genius; and for the death of few
public men,
was public grief ever more sincere.
When these grounds were proposed, he was at once
called to design them;
but, before they were completed, he perished in the wreck of the
steamer Henry Clay.
His mind was singularly just, penetrating, and original.
His manners were calm, reserved, and courteous.
His personal memory
belongs to the friends who loved him;
his fame to the country which honored and laments him.

On the west side :—

I climb the hill from end to end:
Of all the landscape underneath
I find no place that does not breathe
Some gracious memory of my friend.

'T is held that sorrow makes us wise;
Yet how much wisdom sleeps with thee,
Which not alone had guided me,
But served the seasons that may rise!

And doubtless unto thee is given
A life that bears immortal fruit,
In such great offices as suit
The full grown energies of Heaven.

And love will last as pure and whole
As when he loved me here in time,
And at the spiritual prime
Reawaken with the dawning soul.

On the south side :—

"The taste of an individual,
as well as that of a nation, will be in direct proportion to the
profound sensibility
with which he perceives the beautiful in natural scenery."

" Open wide, therefore,
the doors of your libraries and picture-galleries,
all ye true republicans !
Build halls where knowledge shall be freely diffused among men,
and not shut up within the narrow walls of
narrower institutions.
Plant spacious parks in your cities,
and unclose their gates as wide as the gates of morning to the
whole people.
[*Downing's Rural Essays.*]

On the east side :—

" Weep no more,
For Lycidas, your sorrow, is not dead,
Sunk though he be beneath the wat'ry floor.
So sinks the day-star in the ocean bed,
And yet anon repairs his drooping head,
And tricks his beams, and with new spangled ore
Flames in the forehead of the morning sky.
So Lycidas sunk low, but mounted high
Through the dear might of Him that walked the waves."

Upon the pedestal of this monument there is an inscription which states that it was erected in September,
1852, by the American Pomological Society.

Nearer to the building is a sarcophagus, which Capt.
J. D. Elliott, U. S. N., under the supposition that it formerly contained the mortal remains of the Emperor
Alexander Severus, took great pains to obtain; and
bringing it to the United States in the frigate Constitution, made a formal tender of it, through the officers of

the National Institute, to General Jackson, as a fitting receptacle for the body of that illustrious President.

The following correspondence took place, and the proposition proving distasteful to General Jackson, the sarcophagus remained for a long period in the basement of the Patent Office, and is now exposed to the inclemency of the atmosphere in the grounds of the Smithsonian Institution : —

NAVY YARD, PHILADELPHIA, *April* 8, 1845.

GENTLEMEN : The interest which the National Institute has been pleased to take in the eventual bestowment of the remains of the Honorable Andrew Jackson, in the sarcophagus which I brought from abroad and deposited in your Institute, makes it my business now to commucate to you a copy of his letter of the 27th ultimo, lately received on that subject. With sentiments so congenial to his strict republicanism, and in accordance, indeed, with the republican feelings common to ourselves, he takes the ground of repugnance to connecting his name and fame in any way with imperial associations. We cannot but honor the sentiments which have ruled his judgment in the case, for they are such as must add to the lustre of his character. We subscribe to them ourselves; and while we yield to their force, we may still be permitted to continue our regard to the enduring marble, as to an ancient and classic relic, a curiosity in itself, and particularly in this country, as the first of its kind seen in our western hemisphere. From it we would deduce the moral, that while we would disclaim the pride, pomp, and circumstances of imperial pageantry, as unfitting our institutions and professions, we would sedulously cherish the simple republican principles of reposing our fame and honors in the hearts and affections of our countrymen. I have now, in conclusion, to say, that as the sarcophagus was originally presented with the suggestion of using it as above mentioned, I now commit it wholly to the Institute as their own and sole property, exempt from any condition.

I am, very respectfully, yours, &c.,

JESSE DUNCAN ELLIOTT.

To the PRESIDENT AND DIRECTORS of the National Institute at Washington.

HERMITAGE, *March* 27*th*, 1845.

DEAR SIR: Your letter of the 18th instant, together with the copy of the proceedings of the National Institute, furnished me by their corresponding secretary, on the presentation by you of the sarcophagus for their acceptance, on condition it shall be preserved, and in honor of my memory, have been received, and are now before me. Although laboring under great debility and affliction, from a severe attack from which I may not recover, I raise my pen and endeavor to reply. The steadiness of my nerves may perhaps lead you to conclude my prostration of strength is not so great as here expressed. Strange as it may appear, my nerves are as steady as they were forty years gone by, whilst from debility and affliction I am gasping for breath. I have read the whole proceedings of the presentation by you of the sarcophagus, and the resolutions passed by the Board of Directors, so honorable to my fame, with sensations and feelings more easily to be conjectured than by me expressed. The whole proceedings call for my most grateful thanks, which are hereby tendered to you, and through you to the President of the National Institute. But with the warmest sensations that can inspire a grateful heart, I MUST DECLINE ACCEPTING THE HONOR INTENDED TO BE BESTOWED. I cannot consent that my mortal body shall be laid in a repository prepared for an emperor or a king—my republican feelings and principles forbid it—the simplicity of our system of government forbids it. Every monument erected to perpetuate the memory of our heroes and statesmen ought to bear evidence of the economy and simplicity of our republican institutions, and the plainness of our republican citizens, who are the sovereigns of our glorious Union, and whose virtue is to perpetuate it. True virtue cannot exist where pomp and parade are the governing passions. It can only dwell with the people, the great laboring and producing classes, that form the bone and sinew of our confederacy. For these reasons I cannot accept the honor you and the President and Directors of the National Institute intended to bestow. I cannot permit my remains to be the first in these United States to be deposited in a sarcophagus made for an emperor or king. I again repeat, please accept for yourself, and convey to the President and Directors of the National Institute, my profound respects for the honor you and they intended to bestow.

I have prepared an humble depository for my mortal body, beside that wherein lies my beloved wife, where, without any pomp or parade, I have requested, when my God calls me to sleep with my fathers, to be laid, for both of us there to remain until the last trumpet sounds to call the dead to judgment; when we, I hope, shall rise together, clothed with that heavenly body promised to all who believe in our glorious Redeemer, who died for us that we might live, and by whose atonement I hope for a blessed immortality.

I am, with great respect, your friend and fellow-citizen,

ANDREW JACKSON.

To Hon. J. D. Elliott, United States Navy.

WASHINGTON ARMORY.

In the act making appropriations for the civil and diplomatic expenses of government, passed by the second session of the 33d Congress, and approved March 3d, 1855, a clause was inserted appropriating $30,000 for the construction, on such site, in a central position on the public ground, in the city of Washington, as might be selected by the President, of a suitable building for the care and preservation of the ordnance, arms and accoutre-

9

ments of the United States, required for the use of the
volunteers and militia of the District of Columbia, the
care and preservation of military trophies, and for the
deposit of newly-invented and model arms.   To this legislation the public are indebted for the grim and solid
building on the Mall, between Sixth and Seventh streets
west, near the Smithsonian Institution.

UNITED STATES ARSENAL.

The United States Arsenal in the District of Columbia
is located in that portion of the city known as " Greenleaf's Point," a position chosen for its stratagetic importance, as it is near the confluence of the Anacostia and
Potomac rivers, where the largest class of shipping can
receive such munitions of war as national exigencies may
require to be despatched.   The buildings were commenced
under the superintendence of Colonel Bomford, in 1814,
and besides the Construction Department, of great interest
to the student of military science, there is a room of
models, in which the visitor will find death-dealing imple-
ments in such number and variety as only the Tower of
London can surpass.

PENITENTIARY OF THE DISTRICT OF COLUMBIA.

By provision of the act of Congress approved May
20th, 1826, the Penitentiary of the District of Columbia
is committed to the superintendence of the Secretary of
the Department of Interior.   By an act passed February
25th, 1831, the national legislature decreed that the President of the United States should be authorized and
required to appoint three commissioners for the purpose
of selecting a proper site in the District of Columbia on

which to erect a penitentiary, and $40,000 were appropriated for the purchase of such site, and for the construction of the necessary buildings. Congress subsequently appropriated, on February 25th, 1831, $36,360 for the completion of the buildings, and, at various periods since, liberal appropriations have been made towards the support of this unfortunately necessary establishment.

MILITARY ASYLUM.

On one of the most beautiful sites in the vicinity of the city, the traveler finds an edifice of singular beauty, surrounded by grounds that could only be kept in such order by the authorities and subordinates of an " old soldier's home." For this beautiful edifice, the patriot and the old soldier are largely indebted to the foresight and philanthropy of General Winfield Scott. Congress, by the act of March 3d, 1851, provided for the establishment of a Military Asylum, for the relief and support of invalid and disabled soldiers of the United States. The Board of Commissioners appointed under the provisions of this act, reported December 31st, 1851, that they had secured temporary places for the reception of such invalids near New Orleans and at Washington, and had purchased a site in the District of Columbia for the permanent establishment of so important an institution. The Military Asylum is governed and controlled by a Board of Commissioners, consisting of the General-in-Chief, Generals commanding the eastern and western divisions, Quartermaster-General, Commissary-General, Paymaster-General, Adjutant-General, and Surgeon-General of the United States Army. The officers in immediate charge of the Asylum are the Governor, Deputy-Governor, Secretary, and Treasurer, who are selected, by the Board of Commissioners, from the officers of the army.

The classes of persons entitled to the benefits of the asylum are:—1. All soldiers and discharged soldiers of the army of the United States who may have served honestly and faithfully for twenty years. 2. All soldiers and discharged soldiers of the regular army, and of the volunteers, who have served in the war with Mexico, and were disabled by disease or wounds incurred in that service, and in the line of their duty, and who are by such disability incapable of further military service. This class includes that portion of the marine corps which served in the war against Mexico. 3. Every soldier and discharged soldier who may have contributed to the funds of the Military Asylum, since the passage of the act to found the same, approved March 3, 1851, according to the restrictions and provisions thereof, and who may have been disabled by disease or wounds incurred in the service and in the line of his duty, rendering him incapable of military service. 4. Every pensioner (whether a regular or volunteer), on account of wounds or disability incurred in the military service of the United States, though not a contributor to the funds of the institution, who shall transfer his pension to the Military Asylum during the period he voluntarily continues to receive its benefits. No provision is made for the wives and children of the inmates of the Asylum, as such relatives are not recognized by law; but to such invalids as can prosecute a trade or handicraft, facilities are afforded for so doing. No deserter, mutineer, or habitual drunkard can be admitted without such evidence of subsequent good service, good conduct, and reformation of character, as the commissioners shall deem sufficient to authorize admission; nor do the provisions of the act to found the asylum apply to any soldier in the regular or volunteer service who shall have been convicted of felony, or other disgraceful or infamous crime of a civil nature, subsequent to his original admission into the service of the United States. All discharged soldiers (regulars, marines, or volunteers) included in any of the above classes, when applying for admission, must state the company and regiment in which they last served, or the name of the captain and colonel, length of service, and whether a pensioner or not, directly to the Secretary of the Board of Commissioners, Washington, D. C., who, in reply, will inform applicants of the decision of the board relative to claims; and when favorable, will furnish the means allowed by the board for the transportation of each from his home to the nearest branch of the asylum. Invalid soldiers, entitled to pensions for disability incurred prior to the Mexican war, and who have served for a period less than twenty years, are required, by the terms of the act founding this institution, to contribute such pensions to the funds of the institution, during the period they may avail themselves of its benefits; those who have served twenty years and upwards do not contribute their pensions to the fund of the institution.

Such invalid soldiers as receive pensions for disability incurred during the late war with Mexico, being contributors to the funds of the Military Asylum, through the contribution levied on the city of Mexico, retain their pensions, as do all who may receive pensions for disabilities incurred since the passage of the act approved March 3, 1851.

Beside certain prize-money, and some other military sources, the Asylum derives a revenue from the contribution of twenty-five cents a month from each of the prospective benificiaries in the United States Army.

COLUMBIAN INSTITUTION FOR THE DEAF, DUMB, AND BLIND.

This philanthropic institution is situated in the north-eastern part of the city, or rather in a suburb, known as "Kendall Green," in close proximity with the National Printing Office and the church of St. Aloysius. The best proof of the efficiency of its conductors and the importance of its objects is afforded in the following statement of Hon. J. Thompson, Secretary of Interior in 1860. The number of pupils taught during the year ending the 30th of June last was thirty, of which twenty-four were mutes and six blind. The receipts of the treasurer were $6,509 26, and the payments by the superintendent were $6,895 60, the excess being met by a balance in his hands on the 30th of June, 1859. The State of Maryland has recently made provision for placing pupils in the institution, and accessions have been received and others are expected from that quarter. Its buildings and grounds are found not to be sufficiently capacious for the attainment of all that is desired in giving instruction in manual labor and the mechanic arts. The reports of the officers do not show the rate of compensation required by the directors from pay-pupils, and those placed in it by the State of Maryland, but the amount received from the United States during the year by the treasurer having been $5,759 26, supporting and educating about twenty indigent pupils from this District, the rate of cost is shown to have been $287 96 for each, which, at this early stage of the history and progress of the institution, may be regarded as very moderate indeed. This result is only attainable because the management of the funds is intrusted to judicious men, who, from motives of Christian benevolence, not only conduct its affairs without cost, but are themselves constantly making private contributions to its resources. In this state of the case, it appears to be a dictate of wisdom, as well as benevolence, that the institution should be favorably regarded by Congress.

The institution is sustained by appropriations from Congress, from the State of Maryland, and by private contributions. It is open to visitors every week-day (except Saturday), between the hours of 9 A. M. and 3 P. M.

GOVERNMENT HOSPITAL FOR THE INSANE.

In 1855, Congress enacted a law providing for the establishment of an Institution to be known as "The Government Hospital for the Insane," and defining its duties to be "the most humane care and enlightened curative treatment of the insane of the army and navy of the United States and of the District of Columbia." A board of visitors, who are to receive no compensation, is appointed by the President of the United States. The Secretary of the Interior is charged with the appointment of a superintendent, who must be a well-educated physician, possessing competent experience in the care and treatment of the insane, and is required to reside on the premises. Private patients belonging to the District may be received into the asylum, by paying the charges appointed by the Board of Visitors.

To this legislation the country is indebted for the magnificent building dedicated to the relief of the various unfortunates who require its assistance. The location is beautiful and commanding, and the accommodations are ample for all the patients that are entitled to admission. The number of inmates has increased from year to year. On the first of July, 1860, there were from the army, 24; from from the navy, 19; from the Soldiers' Home, 4; and from civil life, 120—total, 167.*

The grounds around the buildings should be laid off and improved, and the entire tract of land substantially inclosed; and for these purposes some additional appropriations will be needed. The institution has heretofore been managed with great efficiency, and bids fair soon to become a model of its kind in every respect.

AMERICAN COLONIZATION SOCIETY.

This society occupies a handsome building, of gray freestone, with iron casings and mouldings, recently erected on the south side of Pennsylvania avenue, at the corner of 4½ street. The Colonization Society was established December 21st, 1816, and chartered by the legislature of Maryland, March 23d, 1837. The government is vested in a board of directors, composed of the life-directors and delegates from the different State societies. The republic of Liberia, on the west coast of Africa, has been formed by the labors of this society. It owns a territory extending about five hundred miles along the coast, and indefinitely in the interior, which was purchased from the natives, who are permitted still to reside upon it, and to become citizens of the republic when sufficiently civilized.

About 200,000 of them reside within the limits of the republic and under its government.

The society has removed from the United States to Liberia 10,545 persons. The present population (American) is not more than this number. The independence of Liberia has been recognized by several of the leading European nations. From its beginning up to January 1st, 1861, the society received from all sources $2,247,407.

UNITED STATES AGRICULTURAL SOCIETY.

This society claims and is entitled to rank with the Royal Agricultural Society of England and the Imperial Agricultural Society of France. The importance of the interests over which it watches was indicated to the foresight of Washington, as is evidenced by his letter to Sir John Sinclair, under date of July 20th, 1794, wherein he says: "It will be some time, I fear, before an agricultural society, with congressional aid, will be established in this country. We must walk, as other countries have, before we can run; smaller societies must prepare the way for greater; but, with the lights before us, I hope we shall not be so slow in maturation as older nations have been. An attempt, as you will perceive by the inclosed outlines of a plan, is making to establish a State society in Pennsylvania, for agricultural improvements. If it succeeds, it will be a step in the ladder; at present, it is too much in embryo to decide upon the result."

Two years afterward, the same eminent authority made the following statement to Congress: "It will not be doubted that, with reference to either individual or national welfare, agriculture is of primary importance. In proportion as nations advance in population and other

9*

circumstances of maturity, this becomes apparent." On the 14th of June, 1852, a National Agricultural Convention was held at the Smithsonian Institution, in the City of Washington, under a call issued by the following agricultural societies, at the instance of the Massachusetts Board of Agriculture: The Massachusetts State Board of Agriculture; Pennsylvania State Agricultural Society; Maryland State Agricultural Society; New York State Agricultural Society; Southern Central Agricultural Society; Ohio State Board of Agriculture; American Institute, New York; Massachusetts Society for the Promotion of Agriculture; Indiana State Board of Agriculture; New Hampshire Agricultural Society; Vermont Agricultural Society; and the Rhode Island Society for the Encouragement of American Industry. This convention resulted in the formation of the United States Agricultural Society, whose permanent office is now in the City of Washington.

NATIONAL PRINTING OFFICE.

In 1860, Congress authorized the Superintendent of Public Printing to negotiate for the purchase or erection of a printing office for the public use. After making the most diligent inquiry, the Superintendent came to the conclusion that his official trust would be best discharged by the purchase of the vast establishment owned by Mr. C. Wendell. In pursuance of the instruction of Congress, he agreed to pay Mr. Wendell $135,000 for his printing office, which is equal in extent to any in the world. This bargain received the indorsement of both branches of Congress in the second session of the thirty-sixth Congress. The immense building which has thus become national, and in which may be found the most recent and perfect machinery belonging to the typographical art, is directly north of the Capitol, and is generally the first remarkable object observed by persons entering the city on the Baltimore Railroad.

WASHINGTON ART ASSOCIATION.

The Constitution of this Association provides for its nationality by declaring that artisans of every profession and vocation, throughout the Union, who are interested in the welfare and honor of their country and in the cause of art, shall be eligible to election as members of the Association. The volume of the Constitution contains a long list of members' signatures—names of men eminent in every department of art, science, literature, instruction, invention, jurisprudence, and statesmanship; names also of noble and accomplished women. It aims at the development and fostering of American genius, and has proposed to itself an immense task.

THE EQUESTRIAN STATUE OF JACKSON.

The Jackson Monument Committee were authorized, by resolution of Congress, dated August 11, 1848, to receive the brass guns captured by Jackson at Pensacola, "to be used as material for the construction of a monument to that distinguished patriot;" the monument to be erected on such portion of the public grounds in the city of Washington as might be designated by the President; and, by acts of July 29 and September 20, 1850, other condemned brass guns were also granted for the purpose, with the privilege of exchange.

Clark Mills was appointed to execute the statue, and

immediately proceeded to model a design, for which purpose he procured and trained the finest breed and build of horses, and made thorough study of the anatomy and pose of the animal, sparing no labor or care in arriving at the precise nature of his subject. He erected his own foundry, being a natural mechanic, and cast the statue himself.

President Fillmore selected the site for the statue, when completed, in the centre of the square in front of the Executive Mansion, where it was inaugurated, January 8, 1853, the anniversary of Jackson's victory at New Orleans, in 1815.

General Jackson is represented in the exact military costume worn by him,—with cocked hat in hand, saluting his troops. The charger, a noble specimen of the animal, with all the fire and spirit of a Bucephalus, is in a rearing posture, poised upon his hind feet, with no other stay than the balance of gravity, and the bolts pinning the feet to the pedestal. The work is colossal, the figure of Jackson being eight feet in height, and that of the horse in proportion. The whole stands upon a pyramidal pedestal, of white marble, seven feet in height, at the base of which are planted four brass six-pound guns, taken by the hero at New Orleans. The cost of the statue to the government, including the pedestal and iron railing, was $28,500.

THE EQUESTRIAN STATUE OF WASHINGTON.

Congress passed an act, as early as 1783, authorizing the erection of an equestrian statue of Washington at the seat of government, and the minister to France was empowered to engage an artist for the work to be done, in

Paris. Houdon was chosen, and made his estimates of the expense, which he forwarded, by Dr. Franklin, to this government. The work was not executed, and the original idea, of an equestrian statue as a national memorial, was changed, in 1832, to that of the obelisk now in course of construction on the Mall.

By act of Congress, passed January 25, 1853, the sum of $50,000 was appropriated, "to enable the President to employ Clark Mills to erect, at the City of Washington, a colossal equestrian statue of George Washington, at such place on the public grounds as shall be designated by the President." Mr. Mills proceeded accordingly to execute the statue, which was inaugurated upon the site selected by President Buchanan, in the open space called the Circle, on Pennsylvania avenue, near Georgetown. The inauguration ceremony took place on the anniversary of Washington's birth-day, February 22, 1860.

Washington is represented as he appeared at the battle of Princeton, where, after attempting several times to rally his troops, he put spurs to his horse and dashed up in the face of the enemy's battery. His terror-stricken charger recoils before the blaze of artillery, while the balls tear up the earth beneath him; but Washington, calm and collected, evinces all the dignity and bravery of the hero, and the firmness of the commander-in-chief, believing himself an instrument in the hands of Providence to work out the great problem of American independence.

WASHINGTON AQUEDUCT.

This vast enterprise has cost the nation nearly three millions of dollars. Some of the difficulties of its construction may be inferred from the following official description of the country through which it passes: "The traveler ascending the banks of the Potomac from Georgetown to the Great Falls, would conclude that a more unpromising region for the construction of an aqueduct could not be found. Supported by high walls against the face of jagged and vertical precipices, in continual danger of being undermined by the foaming torrent which boils below, the Canal (the Chesapeake and Ohio) is a monument of the energy and daring of our engineers. The route appears to be occupied, and no mode of bringing in the water, except by iron pipes secured to the rocks, or laid in the bed of the canal, seems practicable. Such were my own impressions; and though I knew that in this age, with money, any achievement of engineering was possible, I thought the survey would be needed only to demonstrate by figures and measures the extravagance of such a work. But when the levels were applied to the ground, I found, to my surprise and gratification, that the rocky precipices and difficult passages were nearly all below the line which, allowing a uniform grade, would naturally be selected for our conduit; and that, instead of demonstrating the extravagance of the proposal, it became my duty to devise a work presenting no considerable difficulties, and affording no opportunities for the exhibition of any triumphs of science or skill."

The conduit is 9 feet in dimension, and discharges 67,596,400 gallons in twenty-four hours. Some idea of the magnitude of the enterprise may be formed by comparing the statement above given with the fact that the Croton aqueduct supplies 27,000,000 gallons, and Philadelphia and Boston are only respectively guaranteed

15,000,000 and 10,176,570 gallons, during the same period.

There are, in all, eleven tunnels, some of them many hundred feet in length, and six bridges. The largest of the bridges is one of the most stupendous achievements of the kind in this country. It spans a small tributary of the Potomac, called the Cabin John creek, by a single arch, 220 feet in span and 100 feet high. The receiving reservoir is formed by throwing a dam across a small stream known as the Powder Mill or Little Falls Branch. The dam is of pounded earth, and floods above 50 acres, making a reservoir of irregular shape, containing, at a level of 140 feet above high tide, 82,521,500 gallons. The water leaves it a distance of 3,000 feet from the point where it enters, and, in slowly passing across this pool, which deepens to 30 or 40 feet near the exit, it deposits most of its sediment. The Powder Mill Branch supplies two or three millions of gallons of pure water daily to the reservoir. The great falls of the Potomac, from whence the supply of water is obtained, are 19 miles distant.

CHAPTER VII.

ETIQUETTE.

———•———
.

POLITENESS and good breeding are the true foundations of social etiquette, and are the same everywhere; yet fashion and position will maintain a controlling influence. At the seat of government, a conventional form of social intercourse seems absolutely indispensable. The idea that there is no rank at our court,—that it is inimical to republican institutions, and that there can, therefore, be no precedence,—has long been exploded by actual experience. The position occupied by officials, under the Constitution, gives them necessarily a certain rank, according to the importance and nature of the office, the length of term, and the age, required by law, of the incumbent. Some officials are permanent residents of Washington, while others remain but a portion of the year. Certain classes are numerous, and others are few in number. The time of some is almost entirely engrossed, while that of others is more at their command. All these circumstances tend to vary the relation between the members of this temporary form of society. Representatives of foreign courts are required, by the laws of international courtesy, to conform to the etiquette of the court at which they are sent to reside, and if there is no established form, they find themselves at a loss in respect of their deportment.

In the early days of our government, foreign customs and forms were tacitly introduced, and although the Jeffersonian dogma of equality was maintained in theory, yet the court etiquette of that period was adhered to with far more dignity and aristocratic precision than exists at present. An order like that of the Cincinnati, would scarcely be tolerated now, although, in the infancy of our government, Washington graced the order as its first president. The avowed object of the order was to establish a rank, without violating the constitution, which prohibits Congress and the States from granting any title of nobility. The following articles were agreed upon during the administration of Washington, and were endorsed by Jefferson :—

In order to bring the members of society together in the first instance, the custom of the country has established that residents shall pay the first visit to strangers, and, among strangers, first comers to later comers, foreign and domestic ; the character of stranger ceasing after the first visits. To this rule there is a single exception. Foreign ministers, from the necessity of making themselves known, pay the first visit to the [cabinet] ministers of the nation, which is returned.

When brought together in society, all are perfectly equal, whether foreign or domestic, titled or untitled, in or out of office.

All other observances are but exemplifications of these two principles.

The families of foreign ministers, arriving at the seat of government, receive the first visit from those of the national ministers, as from all other residents.

Members of the legislature and of the judiciary, independent of their offices, have a right as strangers to receive the first visit.

No title being admitted here, those of foreigners give no precedence.

Differences of grade among the diplomatic members gives no precedence.   .

At public ceremonies, to which the government invites the presence of foreign ministers and their families, a convenient seat or station will be provided for them, with any other strangers invited and the families of the national ministers, each taking place as they arrive, and without any precedence.

To maintain the principle of equality, or of *pêle mêle*, and prevent the growth of precedence out of courtesy, the members of the executive will practice at their own houses, and recommend an adherence to the ancient usage of the country, of gentlemen in mass giving precedence to the ladies in mass, in passing from one apartment where they are assembled into another.

This code of equality was too republican and arbitrary in theory to meet the necessities of the case. The landmarks set by honest pride, to distinguish real inequalities of position, are not so easily obliterated. It is impossible, even, to contravene the established usages of foreign courts, by reversing the relations existing by law, birth, merit, and concession, between foreigners residing here in a representative capacity. The consequence has been that natural distinctions have been maintained, but with some evidence of a disposition on the part of certain classes to deny others' rights which they have no grounds to claim themselves. During President Monroe's first term, there was much excitement in the official coteries upon this subject, which created some hard feeling, as well as many facetious remarks. At the commencement of the session of 1819–20, John Quincy Adams, then Secretary of State, addressed a letter on the subject to Daniel D. Tompkins, Vice-President, wherein he stated that he had been informed by Senators "of a minute of a rule agreed upon, not officially, but privately, by the members of the Senate of the first Congress, that the Senators of the United States paid the first visit to no person except the President of the United States." He repudiated the claim on the part of the Senators, and expressed his intention to make no first calls as being due from him or his family. The letter caused some severe animadversions upon the writer's aristocratic views of society, but the etiquette of the official circles assumed the forms naturally prescribed by the rank and circumstances of the parties interested. There was, lately, some little dissension and confusion regarding the proper forms, but all parties were consulted, and the nature of their rights carefully considered, with a view to the peculiarities of their residence, number, and legal rank. The code was prepared advisedly, and the vexed question adjusted in the revival and establishment of the old usages and customs, which have been founded upon reason and natural privilege, and which have generally prevailed since the foundation of the government.

At the commencement of Washington's first term of administration, he addressed letters to Messrs. Adams and Hamilton, asking their attention and advice upon certain points of etiquette touching the deportment of the President of the United States. A medium between the requirements of the dignity of the office and republican equality was resolved upon, and has remained the rule.

THE CODE.

The President.—Business calls are received at all times and hours, when the President is unengaged. The morning hours are preferred. Special days and evenings are assigned, each season, for calls of respect,—one morning and evening a week being usually assigned for this purpose.

Receptions are held, during the winter season, gene-ally once a week, between eight and ten o'clock in the evening, at which time guests are expected in full dress, and are presented by the usher.

The President holds public receptions on the first of January and the fourth of July, when the Diplomatic Corps present themselves in court costume, and the officers of the Army and Navy in full uniform. The Executive, Legislative, and Judicial branches of the govern-ment are received between the hours of eleven and twelve, after which, the Diplomatic Corps, officers of the Army and Navy, and civilians *en masse*.

The President accepts no invitations to dinner, and makes no calls or visits of ceremony; but is at liberty to visit, without ceremony, at his pleasure.

An invitation to dinner at the President's must be accepted, in writing, and a previous engagement cannot take precedence.

The address of the Executive, in conversation, is, *Mr. President*.

The Vice-President.—A visit from the Vice-President is due the President, on the meeting of Congress. He is entitled to the first visit from all others, which he may return by card or in person.

The Supreme Court.—The Judges call upon the Presi-dent and Vice-President annually, upon the opening of the court, and on the first day of January.

The Cabinet.—Members of the President's Cabinet

call upon the President on New Year's day and the fourth of July. First calls are also due from them, by card or in person, to the Vice-President, Judges of the Supreme Court, Senators, and the Speaker of the House of Representatives, on the meeting of Congress.

The Senate.—Senators call, in person, upon the President and Vice-President, on the meeting of Congress and first day of January; and upon the President on the fourth of July; if Congress is in session. They also call in person or by card, upon the Judges of the Supreme Court, and the Speaker of the House of Representatives, on the meeting of Congress.

The Speaker of the House of Representatives.—The Speaker calls upon the President on the meeting of Congress, first day of January, and the fourth of July, if Congress is in session. The first call is also due from him to the Vice-President, on the meeting of Congress.

The House of Representatives.—Members of the House of Representatives call, in person, upon the President, on the first day of January, and upon the Speaker of the House at the opening of each session. They also call, by card or in person, upon the President on the fourth of July, if Congress is in session, and upon the President, Vice-President, Judges of the Supreme Court, Cabinet officers, Senators, Speaker of the House, and foreign Ministers, soon after the opening of each session of Congress.

Foreign Ministers.—The Diplomatic Corps call upon the President on the first day of January, and upon the Vice-President, Cabinet officers, Judges of the Supreme Court, Senators, and Speaker of the House, by card or in person, on the first opportunity after presenting their credentials to the President. They also make an annual call of ceremony, by card or in person, upon the Vice-President, Judges of the Supreme Court, Senators, and Speaker of the House, soon after the meeting of Congress.

The Court of Claims.—The Judges of the Court of Claims call, in person, upon the President, on the first of January and the fourth of July. They also make first visits to Cabinet officers, and the Diplomatic Corps, and call, by card or in person, upon the Judges of the Supreme Court, Senators, Speaker and members of the House, soon after the meeting of Congress.

The Families of Officials.—The rules which govern officials are also applicable to their families, in determining the conduct of social intercourse.

CHAPTER VIII.

CITY OF WASHINGTON.

————•————

In order to preserve unity in the discussion of our theme, it became necessary to record the most important events in the history of the city under the caption of History of the Seat of Government (Chapter II.); by turning to page 43, therefore, the reader will find what in strictness may be regarded as a portion of the present chapter.

After the conclusion of peace between the United States and Great Britain, in 1814, the necessity for the rebuilding, in the city of Washington, of the edifices of the national government was introduced into the deliberations of the American Congress. An effort to remove the seat of government from its present location was introduced, but met with the fate of similar and subsequent propositions, and resulted in a signal failure. From that time onward, except during the periods of excitement caused by prospective changes of political power growing out of several presidential elections, the value of real estate in the city has gradually increased. Physically, the city has constantly improved, from the grading of streets, and consequent drainage of swamps and pools, until it has become one of the most salubrious cities in the United States. At the commencement of its corporate history, Washington was governed by a board of Com-

missioners; next by a Superintendent, who was the proto-
type of the Commissioner of Public Buildings; then by a
Mayor appointed by the President; and afterwards, under
a charter conceived in a more liberal spirit, by a Mayor
elected by the people every two years, and by two
branches of the municipal council.

We feel compelled, by common dictates of justice, to
explode the fallacy of two ideas which have been generally
entertained. It is supposed that Washington, or the
residents of Washington, have spurned the moral laws
which govern all well-ordered and Christian communities;
and the feeblest attempts at wit ever perpetrated have
attempted to cast ridicule upon the magnificent proportions of a political capital, which was designed upon a
scale drawn from the potential necessities of a nation whose
greatness even the present generation has only faintly conceived. It is well to bear in mind that the march of the
city in population and magnificence has kept steady lock-
step with the advance of national power and population.
With regard to morals, it is not to be denied that Washington is the abode of a legion of foul vices; but this is a
matter, not of reproach to its permanent residents, but of
shame to every patriot; and will be cured when THE PEO-
PLE of every large city, and of each remote hamlet, shall
have acquired a proper reverence for their liberties, a due
conviction of the sanctity of their political duties, and
shall have determined to exercise a vigilant and inflexible
purpose to commit their interests to none but the wisest,
best, and purest of their fellow-citizens. When this shall
have been attained, Washington will cease to bear an undeserved reproach, and will have less cause to regret the
presence of the camp-followers of Congress.

THE CITY HALL.

This imposing building, situated on Judiciary Square, —which is bounded on the east by Fourth street, on the west by Fifth street, on the north by H street, and on the south by the junction of D street and Louisiana and Indiana avenues,—was originally proposed to be erected from the proceeds of a lottery. The cost of its erection has been shared in a near equality between the city and federal government, and as the latter has had an equal use of its accommodations, it is surprising that Congress has exhibited so marked a reluctance to aid in the completion of the building. It will scarcely be credited that the titles to property in the District of Columbia, bills of sale, mortgages, and other records, of vast public and private importance, are daily *and nightly* exposed to the pilfering, or confided to the honor, of any scoundrel who may choose to enter a public, unguarded passage-way, and decide whether or not to mutilate them. The Commissioner of Public Buildings has repeatedly called the attention of Congress to the necessity, upon the ground of national accommodation, for the extension of the City Hall and national court-rooms; and yet the federal legislature has not seen fit to make the necessary appropriation. In its present contracted space, the City Hall contains the office of the Mayor, the rooms used by the Board of Aldermen and City Council, the various local courts of the District, and the Criminal and Circuit Courts of the United States held in the District. The extension of the building is imperatively demanded by the public exigencies; and, when finished, it will be one of the finest architectural adornments within the city limits.

10

WASHINGTON INFIRMARY.

Immediately north of the City Hall is the Washington Infirmary, in which government patients, to the number of nearly a thousand annually, receive the benefit of the best medical treatment. Besides these, there are other patients from public and private sources. The nursing of the sick is confided to the charitable devotees known as Sisters of Charity, but no sectarian predominance is recognized, either in the requisites for admission, or the spiritual advisement of those who are placed in charge of this most laudable institution.

COUNTY JAIL.

This miserable structure, still northward of the Washington Infirmary, is as deficient in all the interior requisites for enabling its faithful officers to perform their duties with an equal regard to the demands of the law and of humanity, as it is devoid of the exterior embellishments to permit us to describe its architecture. Unquestionably, a better building, in a better situation, must soon replace this paltry structure. In the meanwhile, the security of those whom the law directs to be kept in confinement, depends less upon the building in which they reside, than upon the most remarkable vigilance and fidelity of their jailers.

CORPORATION ALMS-HOUSE.

The handsome edifice dedicated to corporate charity, and the restraint and reformation of petty offenders, occupies an elevated site, east of the Capitol, and is a rare specimen of the right building in the right place. Its architecture is pleasing and durable, without unnecessary expense; and a visit to it will quicken the heart and gratify the taste.

WASHINGTON HOTELS.

The hotels of Washington have submitted to a great amount of undeserved abuse from abroad, but they present more features of interest than any similar establishments in the country; for here you meet, not only those who come to buy and sell, and to discuss the rise or fall of stocks, but those whose traffic is with national affairs. The Washington hotels are generally well kept, and if not able to fully accommodate the occasional influx of thousands, it should be remembered that they are built and maintained, not for transient inroads of the masses, but for the accommodation of an average number of guests.

National Hotel.—This is the largest hotel in the city, and one of the largest in the country. It is situated on Pennsylvania avenue, at the corner of Sixth street, and occupies the entire depth of the block. The old National is the stamping-ground of politicians, and the grand centre of political intrigue. Its crowded halls and gay saloons and parlors are proverbial among old frequenters of the seat of government; while its proximity to the Capitol, and excellent management, render it the most favored hotel in Washington.

Willards' Hotel.—This fine edifice is situated on the corner of Pennsylvania avenue and Fourteenth street, and extends to F street, occupying about half of the entire block. The architecture of the building is good, especially that of the modern portion.

Brown's Hotel.—This hotel has a fine marble front on

Pennsylvania avenue, and completes our list of the leading hotels. There are many other excellent establishments for the entertainment of visitors, but as we are not preparing a directory, we must leave the subject.

CHURCHES.

There is little to be said of the ecclesiastical architecture of Washington; it is so generally bad that to particularize one or two decent buildings would be to cast a heavy odium upon all the others. As there is nothing to be said of the buildings, we shall content ourselves with indicating their locality.

Roman Catholic.—St. Patrick's, F street north, near 10th street west. St. Matthew's, H street north and 15th street west. St. Mary's (German), 5th street west, near H street north. St. Peter's (Capitol Hill), 2d street east. St. Dominick's (Island), F street, near 7th street.

Protestant Episcopal.—St. John's, H street north and 16th street west. Epiphany, G street north, near 13th street west. Ascension, H street north, near 10th street west. Trinity, C street north and 3d street west. Grace (Island), D street, near 9th street. Christ Church (Navy Yard), G street south, near 7th street east.

Methodist Episcopal Churches.—Wesley chapel, F street north and 5th street west. McKendree chapel, Massachusetts avenue, near 10th street west. Foundry chapel, 14th street west, near G street north. Union chapel, 20th street, near Pennsylvania avenue. Fletcher chapel, New York avenue and 4th street west. Ryland chapel (Island), Maryland avenue and 10th street. Gorsuch chapel (Island), 4½ street west, near M. Providence chapel (Capitol Hill), J street east and Delaware avenue. Ebenezer, 4th street east, near G street south.

Methodist Episcopal (South).—The only church of this denomination is in a flourishing condition. At present the church edifice is situated on 8th street west, near H street north, but a very fine building will soon be erected on the corner of E street north and 9th street west, and will record the services of a most devoted layman, to whom it owes its existence.

Methodist Protestant.—Chapel on 9th street west, near E street north. Mission Church (Navy Yard), 5th street east and Virginia avenue.

Presbyterian.—First Presbyterian, 4½ street west, near C street north. Second Presbyterian, I street north and New York avenue. Fourth Presbyterian, 9th street west, near G street north. Sixth Presbyterian (Island), 6th street and Maryland avenue. Seventh Presbyterian (Island), 7th street, near D street. Western Presbyterian, G street north, near 19th street west. Assembly's church, I street north and 5th street west.

Baptist.—First church, 10th street west, near F street north. Second church (Maryland), Virginia avenue and 7th street east. Third church, E street north, near 6th street west. Fourth church, 13th street west, near H street north.

Lutheran.—English, H street north and 11th street west. German Evangelical, G street north and 20th street west. Augsburg Confession (German), 4th street west and E street north.

Friends.—I street north, near 20th street west.

Unitarian.—D street north and 6th street west.

Universalist.—Location of church edifice not yet decided upon.

New Jerusalem.—North Capitol street, near B street south.

Synagogue of Israelites.—Location of building not yet decided upon.

Churches of colored congregations.—Asbury, Methodist Episcopal, 11th street west and 3d streeth north. Little Ebenezer, Methodist Episcopal, C street south, near 5th street east. Israel Bethel, African Methodist Episcopal, Capitol street south. Union Bethel, African Methodist Episcopal, 15th street west and M street north. Zion Wesley, (Island), D street, near 3d. First Colored Baptist, 19th street west and I street north. Second Colored, Missouri avenue, near 7th street. Colored Presbyterian, 15th street west, near J street north.

COLLEGES.

Near the northern boundary of the city, on Fourteenth street, is situated one of the most influential and respectable colleges in the country. From Columbia College have graduated some of the brightest lights in the law, theology, and science; and we should do great injustice to its accomplished faculty if we contented ourselves with a description of the inappropriate building in which so much intellectual service is performed. The location is one of the most beautiful and healthful in the District of Columbia, and the view from the college, to the southeast, such as only the pencil of a master could delineate. The college was incorporated in February, 1821, the land having been purchased in 1819, the building commenced in 1820, and the first President elected in 1821. Connected with the college are two literary societies, one of which possesses a library of two thousand volumes. The college library contains five thousand volumes.

National Medical College.—This medical school is a department of Columbia College, and possesses facilities for medical instruction equal to those of any similar institution in any city of the Union. Being under the same roof with the Washington Infirmary, the opportunities for thorough clinical illustration are very great. The location of the college, at the seat of the national government, affords extraordinary advantages to the student who wishes to prosecute any of the collateral branches of science; for here the most numerous sources of scientific improvement are gratuitously open to the student. The libraries of Congress, the Smithsonian Institution, and the Patent Office, enriched with rare and costly works in medicine, as well as the best volumes in all the departments of science and literature, afford opportunities for the profitable employment of hours of leisure from professional study. Added to these advantages, lectures are delivered during the winter upon various branches of science, and the student can listen to them without charge, and without interfering with his legitimate studies. Even in a local point of view, medical instruction is of some consequence, as will be seen by the fact that there are enrolled, in the membership of the medical practitioners recognized by the Medical Society, 81 physicians in Washington, and 10 in Georgetown.

Gonzaga College, under the direction of the Roman Catholic Church, is situated on F street north, near Tenth street west, and has earned a good reputation in conse-

quence of the faithfulness of its large corps of instruct-
ors.

WASHINGTON JOURNALS

From various causes, but principally because of the tele-
graphic connection between the seat of government and the
city of New York, the local support of newspapers published in Washington is generally of less value to them than
official and congressional patronage. Because of this,
there is a risk in recording titles, with the exception of
the *National Intelligencer*,—which, having lived so long,
seems likely to endure forever,—and the *Globe*, which,
as the record of the debates in Congress, must always
continue, under that or some other designation. The
former was established, as a tri-weekly sheet, by S. H.
Smith and Joseph Gales, the latter of whom for
some time discharged the duty of reporter to Congress, in
the performance of which labor twenty. persons are now
employed by one newspaper. Mr. Gales died in 1860,
and the entire management of the conservative and con-
scientious journal devolved upon Mr. W. W. Seaton,
who, for more than half a century, has labored regularly
and incessantly to sustain the unblemished character of
the *Intelligencer*. It is a fine specimen of a journal,
which, dispensing with the anticipation of news, records,
after investigation and deliberation, the "very age and body
of the times;" the history of the United States, during
the existence of the *National Intelligencer*, could easily be
compiled from its columns. The *Globe*, as intimated
above, is the official organ for reporting the debates in
Congress, and is almost entirely devoted to that object.
There are other newspapers, as the *Star*, the *States*, and

the *Republican.* Foremost amongst those whose literary gifts and attainments have contributed to enrich the periodical literature of Washington, is John Savage, Esq., whose productions, in poetry, prose, and dramatic writing, have given him a wide and well-earned fame.

LIBRARIES AND ART-COLLECTIONS.

Washington Library.—The Washington Library Association was formed in the year 1811. On the 18th of April, 1814, Congress passed an act incorporating the society, under the name of "The Washington Library Company;" and, by a joint resolution, passed March 3, 1823, granted to the company a copy of the Laws of the United States, the Journals of Congress, documents, and State papers then published, and such as should be published thereafter by Congress. The charter intrusts the management of the library to seven directors, elected annually, by shareholders, on the first Monday of April. The shares are six dollars each, and the use of the library is granted to persons not holding shares for three dollars per annum. The library received a donation, from Dr. J. C. Hall, of the collection of Dr. Laurie, numbering about 1,000 volumes. The present extent of the library is about 15,000 volumes.

The company owns a building and lot of ground on Eleventh street, south of Pennsylvania avenue

The library is kept open every day and evening, excepting Sunday.

Library of Peter Force, Esq.—This private collection of books forms the most complete library upon American history in the world. The able and devoted collector has spent a life in gathering up the records of American

10*

history, in all their minutiæ; and this invaluable mine of treasures contains over 50,000 books, pamphlets, newspapers, and manuscripts. The library is situated on the corner of Tenth and D streets, and every student in history is made welcome to its resources by the politeness of its owner.

Collections of Paintings.—Mr. W. W. Corcoran, a munificent patron of art, possesses an invaluable collection of paintings and statuary, a view of which may be obtained on Tuesday and Friday of every week. Here may be seen Powers' "Greek Slave;" "Milton at the Organ," painted by Leutze; "Attack of the Huguenots," by W. D. Washington; "Autumn Scene," by Doughty; and some of the finest productions, principally of American artists, whom Mr. Corcoran has generously patronized and aided.

Nothing can afford better evidence of this gentleman's love for art, whose gallery we have thus hastily noticed, than the fact he has recorded in stone and brick, in the form of a magnificent structure on the corner of Pennsylvania avenue and Seventeenth street. This edifice,—which is one of the best specimens of architecture in the city, and has been erected and dedicated to art,—as long as its grand proportions endure, will testify to the true public spirit of the donor.

Another generous patron of the fine arts, and a connoisseur who deserves the wealth dispensed by him so lavishly upon things of beauty, which, when possessed, are not churlishly hidden from those who have not the same means, is Mr. J. C. Maguire, in whose collection of paintings, to say nothing of the innumerable articles of vertu and literary curiosity, are some very rare gems. Unfor-

tunately for us, the publishers, who have an inalienable
right to literary despotism, and, if not the foes of authors,
are the censors of literary limits, have so hedged us in
that we can give only a hasty glance at the numerous art
treasures in the possession of Mr. Maguire, whose hospitable doors are always open to artists and lovers of art.
In view of our amenability to the chancery of art, however, we dare not omit a reference to a landscape by Paul
Weber, which we venture to pronounce equal in drawing
and color to any American picture ever painted. It is
so full of delicate touches that, after looking at it for a few
moments, you expect to see the cattle step out of the
canvas and frame. The rivulet winding down the mount-
ain was never done by any but a master's hand. And
right here we must take the liberty to introduce into our
theme an artistic suggestion. We hear a great deal said,
amongst artists and connoisseurs of art, about "old masters," and it is suggested that an old master is no better
than a new master. But it ought to be borne in mind
that what are technically described as "old masters," are
those whose industry and excellence were so great that
their works have outlived those of their cotemporaries.
No doubt there were many artists who executed paintings
and sculpture at the date of those works we now seek
so anxiously as the productions of "old masters," but
we are eager to obtain the works of old masters of excellence; we seek for their works not because of their
date, but for their beauty. Thus, there are many men
and women who can now paint tolerable horses and
dogs, but three centuries hence these may be forgotten,
and Rosa Bonheur and Landseer counted more valuable
than gold or diamonds. In the collection of Mr. Maguire

there is a rare masterpiece, which, from its attribute, only
to be discovered after long examination, proves to be a
head of St. Paul, by an old master. It is probably by
Rubens, but it may be a Veronese. Nothing can be
finer than the "Study of Cattle," by Delatrie, the Ma-
donna de la Peche, or the "Head of Danae," by Wert-
muller. Many other pictures in this collection would
enable us to fill many pages of description, which we
regret we are compelled to abandon.

Mr. Janvier's collection is very rich, and was obtained
by its possessor during several years' residence in Italy.
Like every lover and friend of art, Mr. Janvier opens his
hospitable door to painter, poet, or lover of art. Among
the most valuable paintings in this collection are, the portrait of Pope Paul III., attributed to Titian; a portrait
of King William III. when a child, in which the artist,
Van der Dom, has gratified his love of allegory by representing the youthful prince as blowing bladders, while before him are the fleeting treasures of money and jewels,
and the more reliable wealth indicated by an open missal;
a portrait of the Duchess de la Valliere, by Mignard,
in which the lips seem about to part, the eyes to
move, and the bosom, of which there is a liberal display,
to heave; and a work of Andrea Vaccaro, the subject of
which is described in the "*Leggende delle Vergine.*"
There are several other pictures the coloring and drawing
of which seem to establish their title to the rank of origi-
nals by old masters.

Mr. King, a veteran artist, has a large collection,
principally of portraits, in his studio on Twelfth street.

The Washington artists, with whom some fine productions have originated, frequently exhibit their works in

the gallery belonging to Philp & Solomons, the room having been constructed with an especial view to their accommodation, and is admirably suited for its purpose.

FRATERNITIES AND BENEVOLENT SOCIETIES.

There are in Washington the usual quantity of charitable organizations, but we are obliged to content ourselves with the simple mention of the Young Men's Christian Association, Columbia Typographical Society, Ladies' Union Benevolent Society, Washington Orphan Asylum (Protestant), St. Joseph's Male Orphan Asylum (R. C.), and St. Vincent's Female Orphan Asylum.

Free and Accepted Masons.—This old and wide-spread fraternity was early established in the District, Washington having served as Master of lodge No. 22, in Alexandria, at one time within the limits of the District. A convention of lodges met in the District, on December 11th, 1810, in which there were representatives of the following lodges :—Brooke Lodge, No. 42, of Virginia, and the following Lodges chartered by the Grand Lodge of Maryland : Federal Lodge, No. 15; Columbia Lodge, No. 35; Washington Naval Lodge, No. 41; and Potomac Lodge, No. 37. From these lodges the Grand Lodge of the District of Columbia was formed, and new charters were issued. Washington Lodge, of Alexandria, was allowed to remain under the jurisdiction of Virginia, owing to the peculiar fact that its charter was granted to George Washington, and the craft were unwilling to cancel the record of the masonic standing of so illustrious a brother. The first lodge established in California was chartered by this Grand Lodge. At present, there are in existence, within the jurisdiction of the Grand Lodge of the District, the following branches of the Order: Washington Commandery of Knights Templar, Columbia and Washington Royal Arch Chapters, and eleven lodges.

Ancient and Accepted Rite.—This branch of freemasonry is governed by a Supreme Council of those possessing the Thirty-Third Degree, which is an exclusive and executive degree, difficult of attainment, and conferred only upon those who, without an application for it, are selected as proper persons to be received into its mysteries. Under this governing body there have been established in the District, a Grand Consistory, Council of Kadosch, and Osiris Lodge of Perfection.

Independent Order of Odd-Fellows.—This Order was first introduced into the District of Columbia, November 26, 1827, by the establishment of Central Lodge, No. 1, in the city of Washington; the Grand Lodge of the District was instituted November 28, 1828. The Encampment, or Patriarchal branch of the Order, was established by the institution of Columbian Encampment, No. 1, in the city of Washington, in January, 1834. The Grand Encampment of the District was instituted at Alexandria, in April, 1846. Upon the retrocession of Alexandria to Virginia, in 1846, the Grand Encampment was removed to Washington. There are four subordinate encampments and thirteen lodges under the Grand Lodge, eleven in Washington and two in Georgetown.

MARKETS.

Washington is supplied with food by four good markets. The one known as the centre market, on Pennsylvania avenue, needs a new building, and the corporation have long promised to provide what would conduce to the comfort and cleanliness of the people, and add much to the beauty of the most prominent part of the main avenue in the city.

CEMETERIES.

The oldest and best known cemetery in the District is called the Congressional Cemetery, because when a member of Congress or a Senator of the United States dies, his memory is perpetuated in this graveyard, by a monument erected at the public expense; and thus a cemetery really belonging to a corporation has become known as, *par excellence*, "The Congressional." The cemetery thus designated is situated about a mile and a half east of the Capitol. The original name of this residence of the dead was the "Washington Parish Burial Ground," and amongst its early promoters, we find the names of Henry Ingle, George Blagden, Griffith Coombe, Samuel N. Smallwood, Frederick May, Peter Miller, J. T. Frost, and Thomas Tingey, all identified with the early history of the seat of government.

Another cemetery, of greater beauty, is called "Glenwood," and is situated about a mile north of the Capitol, and in a few years will become one of the best improved in the country, its natural advantages only needing time and labor to improve them.

POLICE.

The guardianship of the city is divided between the municipal police and the Auxiliary Guard, who, contrary to the usages of other cities, do not separately patrol the entire city, but are to be found in bodies at the most public places.

TRAVELING FACILITIES.

Washington is connected with the North and West by railroad and canal, and the beautiful Potomac bears the traveler to Alexandria or Acquia creek, where another railroad connection conveys him southward. Between Washington and Alexandria there is an hourly communication by omnibus, and a railroad commencing on the Virginia side of the Long bridge, which spans the Potomac. Besides these principal channels of locomotion, there are the usual stage-coach accommodations for reaching the surrounding country, while two lines of omnibuses convey passengers from Georgetown to the Capitol, or from any part of Seventh street to the Navy Yard. A city railroad is so greatly needed, that the strife for the pecuniary profits to accrue from it cannot much longer prevent its construction.

CHAPTER IX.

GEORGETOWN.

————

THE city of Georgetown is situated on the Potomac, three miles west of the Capitol, and only separated from the city of Washington by Rock Creek, which is spanned by a beautiful iron bridge, constructed on a novel plan. The city is located upon high ground, and commands a beautiful prospect of the Capital and the valley of the Potomac. It was laid out by an act of the colonial government of Maryland, passed June 8th, 1751, and was incorporated by act of the general assembly of Maryland, passed December 25, 1789. It is a port of entry, and carries on a considerable foreign and coasting trade; and is, also, the greatest shad and herring market in the United States, large quantities of these fish being caught in the Potomac and brought here for barreling. The flouring business is extensively carried on, and keeps about fifty mills in constant operation. Manufacturing has also been introduced, and has lately become an important branch of industry. The Chesapeake and Ohio Canal is carried over the Potomac at this place, upon an aqueduct 1,446 feet long and 36 feet high, costing, in its construction, two million dollars. There are eight churches in the city, two banks, a college, a nunnery, and several hotels. A line of two steamers has lately been established between this port and

New York, for carrying freight and passengers. There is one newspaper in the place, the *Georgetown Advocate*, published tri-weekly and weekly. The population is about eight thousand. A line of stages runs every three minutes between this city and the Capitol, making it convenient for persons doing business in Washington, and members of Congress, to reside here and enjoy the salubrious air and quiet retirement of the place.

GEORGETOWN COLLEGE.

This institution of learning was established in 1791, by the Roman Catholics, under the auspices, and at the suggestion, of the Rev. John Carroll. The buildings were commenced in 1788, and completed in 1795, but the terms opened before the buildings were finished, in 1791. Professors were selected from the Jesuits who sought an asylum in this country from European persecution. The system of education adopted is one long tried and fully approved, being the *ratio dicendi et discendi* of Père Jouvency, and keeps pace with the spirit of development and genius of our age and country,—embracing all literature and modern inventions, and cherishing the principles of liberty and republicanism. The morality of the college is preserved with the most vigilant solicitude ; the nature of the system precluding almost the possibility of the pupils contracting any vicious habits. The seclusion of the site, vigilance of the prefects, and attendance of the professors in their walks within the college grounds, keep the students under a decorous restraint.

The local advantages yield to none in any country ; elevated and sequestered, though within the limits of the town, it lifts its turrets high above the forest that surrounds it, commanding a view of the Potomac, on whose banks it is situated, of the bridge which spans the waters, Analostan Island, the Capitol, and the city of Washington. The prospect in the rear is perfectly rural, varied with hill and dale, and deeply set with every species of forest trees, embowering a serpentine walk which forms a delightful promenade, reminding the contemplative student of the vale of Tempe, while the gurgling stream which meanders through its shades recalls in fancy the waters of Peneus,

Ab imo
Effusus Pindo spumosis volvitur undis.

The library comprises about twenty-five thousand volumes of rare and well-selected works, among which are many of very ancient date, as well as manuscripts and illuminated missals of the middle ages. There is a fine museum attached to the college, and also an astronomical observatory. A vineyard is cultivated on the premises, which supplies the chapel with wine for the altar, and the table of the clergy. The medical department of the institution was organized in May, 1851, under the act of Congress passed in March, 1815, granting the college the rights and privileges of a University. The academic year is from the 15th of September to the 31st of July.

THE CONVENT OF THE VISITATION.

The convent, in Fayette street, is of the order of the Visitation, founded, in 1610, by Saint Francis de Sales, and first superintended by Saint Jane Frances Fremiot de Chantal. The objects of the order are female instruction and the practice of charity. This convent was established, under the diocese of Baltimore, in 1799; and the sisters conduct a female seminary, called the Academy of the Visitation, which is an excellent institution of its kind, and accommodates about two hundred pupils, of all religious denominations, and the course of instruction is very complete, and judiciously chosen.

A public exhibition is given at the close of each academic year, when premiums are awarded to the successful competitors for honors. The annual vacation commences with the exhibition, on the last Thursday of July. The terms for board and tuition are $200 for the annual term. Visitors are admitted to the convent and academy on week-days, between the hours of eleven and two o'clock.

THE CHESAPEAKE AND OHIO CANAL.

The States of Maryland and Virginia, in the year 1784, incorporated a company for the improvement of the river Potomac, the great object of which was to open to the commerce of the seat of government the mineral riches of the Alleghany mountains.

In November, 1823, a convention of delegates from Maryland, Virginia, Pennsylvania, Ohio, and the District of Columbia, met in Washington, for the purpose of calling the attention of government to this important project. On the 28th of May, 1828, Congress passed an act appropriating $1,000,000, but specifying that the canal should be sixty feet wide and six feet deep. The City of Washington subscribed $1,000,000, and Alexandria and Georgetown $250,000 each ; Virginia, $250,000 ; and Maryland, $5,000,000.

The ground was broken, for the commencement of the work, on the 4th of July, 1828, on which occasion John

Quincy Adams, then President of the United States, officiated in the performance of the ceremony. The canal
extends to Cumberland, a distance of one hundred and
eighty-four miles, and is supplied with water from the
Potomac, by means of dams.

The entire cost of the work was about $12,000,000.

OAK-HILL CEMETERY.

This beautiful place was laid out, and presented to the
shareholders of the District of Columbia, by W. W. Corcoran, Esq., the beneficent banker. It is situated on the
heights of Georgetown, upon the western slope of the
banks of Rock Creek, and is beautifully laid out in ter-
races and walks, overshadowed by tall oak trees. The
ground is varied by hill and dale, and commands most
charming views of the exquisite scenery of the valley of
the stream, broken into vistas and secluded nooks by the
undulating and varied nature of the ground. There are,
already, many grand monuments erected here, and numerous vaults prepared for the wealthier families of the District. The vault belonging to the donor, Mr. Corcoran,
stands upon the brow of the hill, in a very conspicuous
and beautiful location, and is surmounted by a primitive
Grecian temple of the Doric order, octagonal in form, and
built of white marble, at a cost of over $25,000. The
granite monument to Bodisco, the late Russian Minister,
is worthy of notice. The shaft was sent from St. Peters-
burgh, by the Russian government. The entrance is
graced by a tasteful Gothic lodge, of sandstone. The
stone chapel, overgrown with ivy, is an attractive and
beautiful feature of the cemetery.

CHAPTER X.

———————◆———————

THE vicinity of the seat of government is full of interest, but our limits will only permit us to mention those
points of attraction which, from historic, as well as common
reputation, cannot be passed over in silence.

•

BLADENSBURGH.

This village is situated on the eastern branch of the
Potomac, in Prince George's County, Maryland, on the
line of the Baltimore and Washington railroad, six miles
northeast of the Capitol, and contains about five hundred
inhabitants. It has many interesting associations with
the seat of government, on account of the battle which
was fought here, in defence of the city of Washington
against the British, in 1814; and also from the painful
reminiscences of the numerous duels fought in its vicinity
since the location of the government in the District. The
old battle-ground is still pointed out to strangers, above
the bridge which crosses the branch, and it is often the
case of pique to the inhabitants of the village when some
bantering wag inquires the way to the " race course."
Soon after the sack of Washington, the following verses

were written upon the four-mile stone, near the site of the defeat :—

> Here fought Commodore Barney,
> So nobly and so gallantly,
> Against Britain's sons and slavery;
> For a fighting man was he!

> There did General Winder flee,
> His infantry and cavalry;
> Disgracing the cause of liberty;
> For a writing man was he!

The Duelling-Ground.—This scene of so many deadly encounters is situated upon the road from Washington to Bladensburgh, about four miles from the city, in an opening of the trees, which shelter the lawn from observation. This sequestered spot was at first chosen for its natural seclusion, and has since been used as a duelling-ground, from custom, and the necessity of evading the act of Congress, passed July 20, 1839, which makes duelling, in the District of Columbia, a penal offence, punishable by ten years' hard labor in the penitentiary.

The first duel of which this ground was the theatre, appears to be that in which Edward Hopkins was killed, in 1814.

In 1819, A. T. Mason, a United States Senator from Virginia, fought, upon this celebrated ground, with his sister's husband, John McCarty. McCarty was averse to fighting, and thought there was no necessity for it; but Mason would fight. McCarty named muskets, loaded with grape-shot, and so near together that they would hit heads if they fell on their faces. This was changed by the seconds to loading with bullets, and taking twelve feet as the distance. Mason was killed instantly, and McCarty had his collar-bone broken. In 1820, Commodore Decatur was here killed in a duel, by Commodore Barron. At the first fire both fell forward, with their heads within ten feet of each other, and, as each supposed himself mortally wounded, each fully and freely forgave the other. Decatur expired immediately, but Barron eventually recovered. In 1822, Midshipman Locke was killed here, by a clerk of the Treasury Department, named Gibson; the latter was not hurt. In 1833, Mr. Key and Mr. Sherborn had a hostile encounter, and, after an exchange of shots, Mr. Sherborn said:—"Mr. Key, I have no desire to kill you." "No matter," said Key, "I came to kill you." "Very well, then," said Sherborn, "I will kill you." And he did. In 1838, W. J. Graves, of Kentucky, assuming the quarrel of James Watson Webb with Jonathan Cilley, of Maine, selected this place for the duel, and Cilley was killed. In 1845, a lawyer named Jones fought with and killed Dr. Johnson. In 1851, R. A. Hoole and A. J. Dallas had a hostile meeting. Dallas was shot in the shoulder, but recovered.

LITTLE FALLS.

Three miles westward from Georgetown, the Potomac forms a succession of cascades, designated the Little Falls. The noble river is at this point beautiful enough to provide immortal fame for the artist who shall properly delineate it. Overlooking its turbulence, the traveler crosses a bridge, the structure of which assures him instinctively of his safety, and he arrives on the Virginia shore. Following the highway for fifteen miles, over picturesque hills and through fine forests, he finds a cross-road, leading to the

GREAT FALLS.

This romantic water-fall, without any pretension to the majesty of Niagara, is a sublime specimen of the wildest mood of nature. Through fierce and jagged barriers of rock, the river forces its imperial march, with such vehemence as seems to involve an immediate agent stronger than the force of gravity; foaming and boiling, the crests of the hurried billows appear to be white masses, hurled by Titanic hands. The whole scene is of that kind called savage, but may be more properly styled regal, nature—or the laws of nature, known and unknown, asserting the supremacy of the original force over all barriers. No theme could be so grand for a poet, no scene more suggestive for a painter; and Mr. W. D. Washington has proved himself a true son of the soil upon which he was born, and a master of the art to which he has devoted himself, by the fine picture he has painted of this contrast of sky, rocks, and water. This point of the river furnishes the water used by the people of Washington, which is conveyed to them by means of the national aqueduct, of which we have previously spoken.

ALEXANDRIA.

The City of Alexandria is distant seven miles from Washington, with which city there is a constant communication by steamboat, omnibus, and railroad. The width of the river, and the depth of its waters, form here a fine harbor for the commerce of this portion of the country; which, although it has not arrived at the greatness anticipated in former years, is still considerable, and is principally employed in the transportation of coal, tobacco, and corn. Railroad and steamboat facilities are

11

afforded for the traveler desiring to proceed in any direction. The site of the city is beautifully undulating. Originally the settlement on this point of the river was denominated "Hunting Creek Warehouse," but some more classical ear insisted upon dubbing it Belle Haven. At one time it had a fair prospect of becoming the seat of government; and so strong was the influence brought to bear in its favor, that it was included in the federal territory, and afterwards returned, by act of Congress, in 1846, to Virginia. In the latter part of his life, George Washington was a pew-holder in Christ Church, and many reminiscences of that great man are preserved in the records of this ancient church, and also in the archives of Washington Lodge, No. 22, of Free and Accepted Masons. Alexandria is connected with Georgetown and the West by a canal, and a considerable manufacturing business is carried on. The handsome court-house of Alexandria county is located here; some fourteen churches, and numerous schools, form the other public buildings.

FORT WASHINGTON.

This military edifice, originally known as Fort Warburton, is about six miles below Alexandria, and generally visited by persons proceeding from the seat of government to Mount Vernon. It is described by General Wilkinson as being, in 1812, a mere water-battery. Since that time it has not improved in its stratagetic importance. It was intended for offensive action only against the river side, and, being under an acclivity, is, of course, of no service in the other direction. During the last war with Great Britain, the town of Alexandria furnished fifteen hundred dollars towards making the fort defensible; but this did not save that town from a forced contribution, nor preserve the Capital of the nation from plunder.

MOUNT VERNON.

This spot, so surrounded by patriotic associations, descended to George Washington from his half-brother, Lawrence Washington, whose title descended from the patent of Lord Culpepper to John Washington, dated 1670. The father of these Washingtons first married Jane Butler, who bore him the son named Lawrence, and subsequently united himself in a second marriage with Mary Ball, who was the mother of George Washington. The Mount Vernon estate was bequeathed by Augustine Washington, who died in 1743, to Lawrence Washington. The last-named person received a captain's commission in one of the four regiments raised in the American colonies to aid Great Britain in her memorable struggle against the combined forces of France and Spain. His duties subsequently brought him in contact with Admiral Vernon, for whom he conceived and always cherished a strong affection; and after his marriage, in 1743, having settled upon what was then known as the Hunting Creek estate, he called it Mount Vernon.

This beautiful estate has been suffered to fall into a sad state of dilapidation, but having at length passed into the hands of the women of America, it will doubtless be made worthy of the sacred ashes which repose in its shades.

The central portion of the mansion was erected by Lawrence Washington, and the wings were added by George Washington. In the main hall is preserved the key of the Bastile, presented by Lafayette to Washington, as a fitting symbol of the triumph of modern political ideas, embodied in the person of Washington, over the barbarous notions of tyranny, so well represented by the most grim and terrible prison of recent ages.

The Tomb of Washington.—While many cities of the old world contended for the honor of Homer's birth-place, the strife of modern cities has been for the entombment of Washington's ashes; and it is not impossible that this far-seeing statesman was governed by other reasons than those dictated by his acknowledged modesty, when, in his last will and testament, dated July, 1799, he directed that his remains should be interred upon the family estate of Mount Vernon, and not removed therefrom. In the succeeding December, his body was borne to the old vault, with the observance of the following order of procession :—

Cavalry, Infantry, and Guard;

Music;

Clergy;

Horse with the General's saddle and holsters;

Colonel Blackburn;

Col. Sims,			Col. Gilpin,
Col. Ramsay,	BODY.		Col. Marsteller,
Col. Payne,			Col. Little.

Principal Mourners;

Lodge No. 22 of Freemasons;

Corporation of Alexandria;

Citizens.

The old family vault, in which the remains were placed, was south of the mansion, and was constructed of freestone, covered with turf. With a wise anticipation of the future importance of his record to the general history of the world, Washington, in his will, expressed his desire for a new mausoleum in the following terms :—

" The family vault at Mount Vernon requiring repairs,

and being improperly situated besides, I desire that a new one of brick, and upon a larger scale, may be built at the foot of what is called the Vineyard Inclosure, on the ground which is marked out, in which my remains, and those of my deceased relatives now in the old vault, and such others of my family as may choose to be entombed there, may be deposited." But for the atrocious attempt to steal, for transportation to a foreign country, the hallowed relics of the great Chief of America, it is possible that his wishes about the entombment of his family would have been neglected. A new tomb having been erected, the sacred remains, deposited in a marble sarcophagus constructed and presented by Mr. Struthers, of Philadelphia, were removed to their present resting-place on the seventh day of October, 1837.

Above the arch of the vault, in which, within full view, are the sarcophagi containing the relics of George Washington and his wife, Martha Washington, is incribed this sentence :—

WITHIN THIS ENCLOSURE REST THE REMAINS OF
GENERAL GEORGE WASHINGTON.*

---

* On his recent tour through this country, the Prince of Wales, in company with the President and his Cabinet, visited this sacred tomb. After expressing his appreciation of the glorious character of Washington, he desired to plant a tree on the spot, in commemoration of his visit; and some horse-chestnuts having been handed to him, he placed them in the earth. He afterwards put a few more in his pocket, with the intention, as he said, of planting them in Windsor Park, on his return home, as another memento of a visit he should ever regard with feelings of peculiar interest. No more touching tribute was ever paid to the memory of the Father of his Country. The grandson of a king who held Washington as a rebel and a traitor, came to his tomb to do reverence to his virtues; and in this modest but most expressive manner, sought to atone for the errors of his ancestors.

11*

The mansion contains many valuable historical relics; amongst which may be mentioned, the key of the Bastile, presented by Lafayette; portions of the military and personal furniture of Washington; the pitcher portrait, on the back of which some one has recorded a highly complimentary inscription.

Thanks to the efforts of the Ladies' Mount Vernon Society, aided by the patriotic eloquence of Edward Everett, this sanctified estate has been secured for the people of the United States. Here, then, amidst the most sacred historical associations, we bid farewell to the reader. Long may the groves of Mount Vernon, and the costly magnificence of the Seat of Government, enable those who speak a common language, belong to a common origin, and are inevitably linked in a common destiny, to dwell together in unity!

INDEX.

PHELAN'S

IMPROVED

Billiard Tables

AND

COMBINATION CUSHIONS.

Protected by Letters Patent, dated Feb. 19, 1856; Oct. 23, 1856;
Dec. 8, 1857; Jan. 12, 1858; Nov. 16, 1858;
March 29, 1859; and Sept. 25, 1860.

The recent improvements in these Tables make them unsurpassed in the world. They are now offered to scientific Billiard Players as combining speed with truth,—never before obtained in any Billiard Table.

Salesroom—Nos. 786 and 788 Broadway, New York.

Manufactory—Nos. 63, 65, 67, and 69 Crosby Street.

PHELAN & COLLENDER,
Sole Manufacturers.

———

Just published, by D. APPLETON & CO.,

THE GAME OF BILLIARDS,

BY M. PHELAN.

Fourth edition, enlarged, revised, illustrated with additional diagrams and a portrait on steel of the author. Price, one dollar, elegantly bound; sent by mail, postage free, on receipt of price.

PHELAN & COLLENDER,
63, 65, 67, and 69 Crosby Street.

M. W. GALT & BROTHER,

354 PENNSYLVANIA AVENUE,

(4 Doors West of Brown's Hotel,) Washington, D. C.,

Dealers in Fine Watches, Diamond and other rich Jewelry, Pure Silver Ware, Paris Fancy Goods, English and American Plated Ware, Guns, Pistols, &c.

☞ A large assortment of Gold, Silver and Fancy Articles, gotten up especially for Presents, Mementoes, and Testimonials.

No. 486.

𝕴𝖓𝖙𝖊𝖗𝖎𝖔𝖗 𝕬𝖉𝖔𝖗𝖓𝖒𝖊𝖓𝖙𝖘.

Paper Hangings, all grades and prices.

Warranted Gold Band Window Shades.

Buff, Green and Blue Holland Shades, all sizes, made to order.

Picture Cord and Tassels, all sizes and colors.

Photograph Frames, different styles and sizes.

Purchasing for cash, and allowing no old stock to accumulate, persons needing the above goods will find it to their advantage to give me a call.

All work executed and superintended by practical men, who have served a regular apprenticeship at their trade.

Satisfaction guaranteed, or no pay required.

Orders punctually executed in city or country.

Remember the number—

JOHN MARKRITER,

No. 486 7th St.,

8 Doors above Odd Fellows' Hall,

WASHINGTON CITY, D. C.

WILLIAM B. WEBB,
ATTORNEY AND COUNSELLOR AT LAW,
No. 4 LOUISIANA AVENUE,
WASHINGTON, D. C.

Practices in the Supreme Court of the United States, the Court of Claims, and the several Courts of the District of Columbia.

UNITED STATES COMMISSIONER.

Brady's National Portrait Gallery,
BROADWAY,

Corner Tenth Street,   NEW YORK.

Branch Gallery, 352 Penn. Ave., Washington, D. C.

GURNEY'S PHOTOGRAPHIC & FINE-ART GALLERY,
707 BROADWAY, N. Y.
1st Block below New York Hotel.

ESTABLISHED 1840.
J. GURNEY.   B. GURNEY.

TESTIMONIALS:

I approve highly of its principles, and recommend it as an important and useful improvement in the treatment of Hernia.　　J. M. CARNOCHAN,
Prof. Surgery N. Y. Med. Col., and Sur. in Chief to State Hos., N. Y.

DR. ARMSTRONG, an eminent Surgeon of Porto Rico, says, "I consider the 'Riggs' Truss' *superior to all others*, and recommend and apply *no other* in my practice."

DR. GOSLING, Shelbyville, Tenn. "The principle of the multipedal Truss is correct, and will accomplish *all that Trusses possibly can do*."

DR. BONTECOW, of Troy. "I wish to introduce them in this city, being convinced they are *superior to all others*."

DR. CRAFTS, Binghampton. "I can truly say the cases I have treated by your Truss promise a cure, and all who are wearing it are highly pleased."

DR. RIGGS'
TRUSS.

Water Proof.

USED IN BATHING.

ALWAYS CLEAN
Never Injures the CORD.

This Truss challenges comparison with any other in the world! Specimens now on hand which have been in constant use from six months to two years.

☞ Young subjects invariably cured.

Office, No. 2 BARCLAY ST., N. Y.

MARBLE HOTEL,

WASHINGTON CITY.

This Hotel is situated on Pennsylvania Avenue, midway between the Capitol, President's Mansion, and Public Departments. The Proprietor having recently erected this magnificent structure expressly for a First-Class Hotel, it is supplied with every convenience and comfort, and furnished equal to any hotel in the United States. For the accommodation of families, particular attention has been bestowed; and the Proprietor hopes to merit a continuance of the extensive patronage with which he has been honored.

THE NATIONAL

Democratic Quarterly Review,

A Periodical of Political, Literary and Scientific Knowledge,

WASHINGTON CITY, D. C.

Contents of No. V., Vol. III., February, 1861:

From Morris & Willis' Home Journal.

Its staff of writers includes some of the first minds in the country, among others, John Savage, Senator Nicholson, Commander Maury, Henry Watterson, J. B. Thorpe, Judge Loring, Caleb Cushing, Professors Henry and Bache, and others eminent in politics and literature, whose combined talent produce an able and interesting "Review."

SUBSCRIPTION PRICE,

Three Dollars per Annum, in advance.

CLUBS, CANVASSERS, POSTMASTERS, AND AGENTS

Will be supplied with the "Review" at the following rates:

For 10 copies per annum,			$27 50
For 20 " "			50 00
For 50 " "			112 50
For 100 " "			200 00

THE CASH TO ACCOMPANY THE ORDER IN ALL CASES.

☞ Address all letters to Hon. T. B. FLORENCE, Washington, D. C.

LITTLE, MORRIS & CO.,
PUBLISHERS.

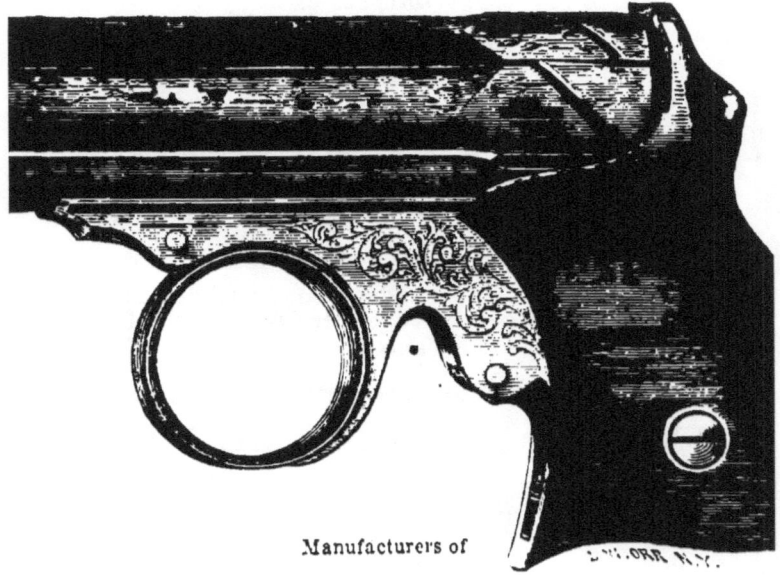

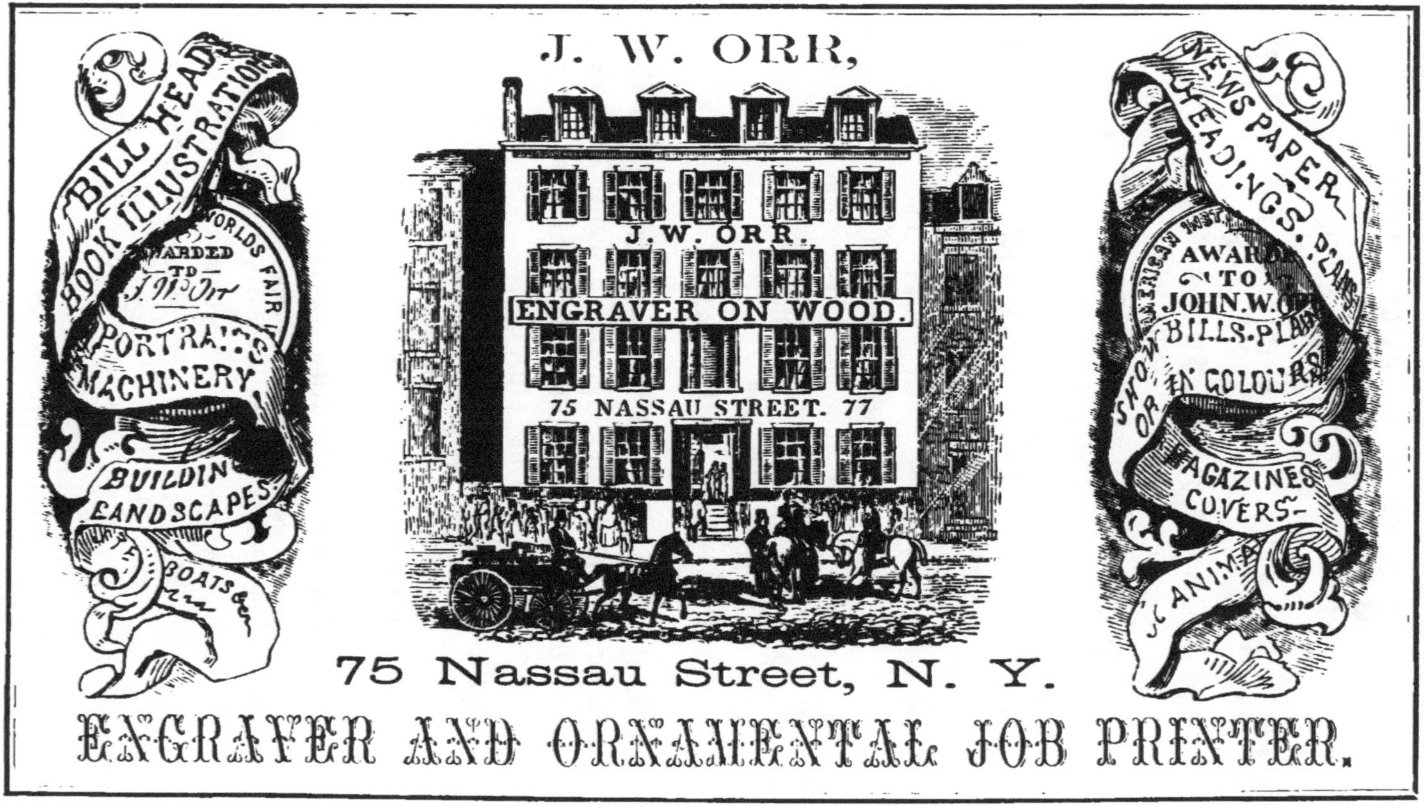

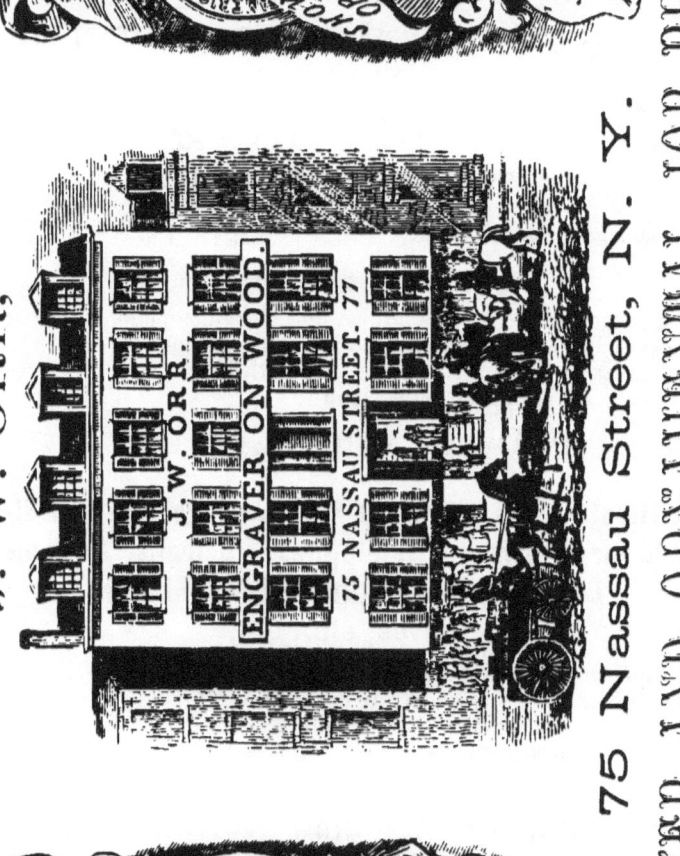

J. W. ORR,
BILL HEADS
BOOK ILLUSTRATIONS
WORLDS FAIR
AWARDED TO J. W. Orr
PORTRAITS
MACHINERY
BUILDIN
LANDSCAPES
BOATS &c
J. W. ORR.
ENGRAVER ON WOOD.
75 NASSAU STREET. 77
NEWSPAPER
HEADINGS. PLAIN
AWARD TO JOHN. W. ORR
SHOW BILLS. PLAIN OR IN COLOURS
MAGAZINES COVERS
ANIMA
75 Nassau Street, N. Y.
ENGRAVER AND ORNAMENTAL JOB PRINTER.

Washington
Philip

www.ingramcontent.com/pod-product-compliance
Lightning Source LLC
Chambersburg PA
CBHW030640030726
47497CB00006B/1878